Rescuing
ROSIE

Books by Jean Ure

BECKY BANANAS,
THIS IS YOUR LIFE!

BOYS BEWARE

BOYS ON THE BRAIN

FAMILY FAN CLUB

FORTUNE COOKIE

FRUIT AND NUTCASE

ICE LOLLY

IS ANYBODY THERE?

JELLY BABY

JUST PEACHY

THE KISSING GAME

LEMONADE SKY

LOVE AND KISSES

OVER THE MOON

PASSION FLOWER

PUMPKIN PIE

THE SECRET LIFE OF
SALLY TOMATO

SECRET MEETING

SECRETS AND DREAMS

SHRINKING VIOLET

SKINNY MELON AND ME

STAR CRAZY ME!

STRAWBERRY CRUSH

SUGAR AND SPICE

The Dance Trilogy in reading order

BORN TO DANCE
STAR QUALITY

SHOWTIME

Special three-in-one editions

THE FLOWER POWER
COLLECTION

THE FRIENDS FOREVER
COLLECTION

THE TUTTI-FRUTTI COLLECTION

And for younger readers

DAISY MAY
DAZZLING DANNY

MONSTER IN THE MIRROR

Rescuing ROSIE

JEAN URE

HarperCollins *Children's Books*

First published in Great Britain by
HarperCollins *Children's Books* in 2021
HarperCollins *Children's Books* is a division of HarperCollins*Publishers* Ltd
HarperCollins Publishers
1 London Bridge Street
London SE1 9GF

www.harpercollins.co.uk

HarperCollins*Publishers*
1st Floor, Watermarque Building, Ringsend Road
Dublin 4, Ireland

1

ISBN 978–0–00–839851–4

Jean Ure asserts the moral right to be identified as the author of the work.

A CIP catalogue record for this title is available from the British Library.

Typeset in Gill Sans by Palimpsest Book Production Limited, Falkirk, Stirlingshire
Printed and bound in the UK using 100% renewable electricity at
CPI Group (UK) Ltd

This boo   :ure

CHAPTER
I

Learning how to ride had been one of my dreams for almost as long as I could remember – ever since I was six years old and Mum and Dad had taken me to the seaside for the day, and there had been a woman on the beach giving pony rides. I had begged to be allowed to have a go! Mum had been a bit nervous because I was really tiny and the pony was quite big so my feet didn't even reach the stirrups, but I wasn't in the least scared. It just felt so right. The pony woman said I had a natural seat, and for ages afterwards I was all puffed up and had these visions of taking part in gymkhanas and winning rosettes. I knew it was only make-believe, like when you pretend you're a celeb and you're being interviewed for an article in some glossy magazine. I mean, for one thing we were living in London at the time and there wasn't a riding stable anywhere near. It wasn't till I was eleven that we came to live in the country – well, Mum and I came to live in the country – and suddenly there were riding stables all over the place! Still, I never seriously thought that I would be able to take lessons.

Mum and Dad having split up, which was the reason Mum had decided to move, we didn't have very much money. Mum works really hard, translating stuff from foreign languages such as Russian – she is very clever, my mum! But, alas, it is not all that well paid. As for my dad, Mum says he is a lost cause. The reason she says that is because he gave up his very important job in London to go and live in Cornwall with a woman called Wanda and do his 'own thing'. Unfortunately, doing his own thing brings in hardly any money at all, so I knew *he* wouldn't be able to pay for my lessons.

And then, yay! A totally brilliant and unexpected thing

 2

happened. A very aged, ancient relative of Mum's died and Mum came into some money! Only a little bit of money, not like people win on the lottery, but enough for Mum to say that at long last I could have my riding lessons. I couldn't wait to tell Katy! Katy lives right next door to us, with her mum. They had only been there a few months. Before that, they had been townies like us, so when we discovered that we were not only at the same school but were even in the same class, we had become best friends immediately.

Now, every Sunday, as soon as we'd had breakfast we would jump on our bikes and ride as fast as we could to the stables. We couldn't wait to get there! In London our mums would never have let us go anywhere on our bikes for fear of all the traffic. I hadn't even had a bike in those days, but when we moved to the country and she saw how quiet it was, Mum had gone on eBay and found me one. Second-hand, but every bit as good as Katy's, which was bright green and brand new. A birthday present from her dad!

The bikes had been Katy's idea, the riding lessons mine. Katy had never even thought about it before, in spite of living in the country. Not that she had been there all that long, but *she* could have had lessons whenever she wanted. No problem! Her dad is a banker and earns simply stacks of money. Stacks and stacks. And because he and Katy's mum are also divorced – which is one of the things that first made me and Katy bond – he spoils Katy rotten. He is always giving her stuff. If she were to ask him for a diamond tiara, he would probably buy one for her, never mind just paying for riding lessons. But, as she said, it would have been totally disloyal to have done it without me. We were best friends; we do things together! That is what being best friends is all about.

Also, though I don't mean to be unfair, I think that secretly she would have been a bit too scared to do it by herself. It was quite funny the first time we went to the stables, though I tried not to giggle because that would have been unkind and might have embarrassed

her. But just for a moment I could almost see her legs turning to jelly. Bethany, the girl who was going to teach us, appeared in the yard leading this enormous great horse towards us. I mean, really huge! It was tossing its mane and making funny snorty noises through its nose. Katy took a step back and went, 'That's n-not for us, is it?' Her voice had gone all thin and quavery. Bethany laughed and said, 'No way! This is Rosie. She's far too big for you.'

I must admit, even I would have found it a bit nerve-racking, climbing on top of a horse that towered way above me! But I reached up and stroked her muzzle and she did the sweetest thing: she pushed her big horsey head into my hand and made this little whickering sound.

'Here,' said Bethany. She dug into her pocket and pulled out a carrot stick. 'Give her this and she'll be yours forever!'

I held it out and that huge great horse took it so gently. All I felt was the soft velvet of her lips brush my hand.

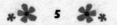

'She's a real sweetie,' said Bethany. 'Aren't you, my darling?'

She put an arm round Rosie and Rosie lowered her head so that Bethany could give her a kiss. I thought, *I could do that!* Not right away, of course; we'd have to get to know each other first. She wouldn't want any old stranger planting kisses on her! Maybe in a week or two she'd feel that I could be trusted. I really, really wanted her to trust me! After all, I wasn't just coming here to learn how to ride; I wanted to learn about the horses themselves. How they behaved, how to look after them, what they enjoyed.

I asked Bethany how long she had been working at the stables and she said that she had been riding there since she was ten years old and now worked part-time in exchange for free rides. I did so envy her!

She told us that in spite of being so big, Rosie was one of the sweetest-natured horses she had ever known.

'Go on!' she said. 'Give her a hug!'

I stood on tiptoe and slipped my arm round Rosie's

neck. Rosie immediately lowered her head and nuzzled at me. I felt so honoured!

Bethany said, 'She just loves being made a fuss of. Katy, go on, you try!'

Poor Katy! I could see she was terrified and trying desperately not to show it.

'She won't hurt you,' said Bethany. 'She'd never do anything to hurt you.'

Very gingerly Katy reached up and patted Rosie's neck. I could see her all tense and holding her breath. Next thing we know she's like, 'Eek!' and falling into a mad fit of the giggles.

'She's chewing my hair!'

'Just nibbling,' said Bethany. 'It's a sign of affection! I told you, she's a real poppet.'

'And so *pretty*,' I said. 'A pink horse!'

Bethany agreed that it was quite an unusual colour. 'She's what's known as a strawberry roan.'

Strawberry roan. I stored it up for future use. It was important to know what I was talking about! Obviously

no real horse person would talk about a horse being *pink*.

Katy, now perfectly relaxed and only too happy to have her hair nibbled, was marvelling at how tall Rosie was. 'She's taller than we are!'

'Almost sixteen hands,' said Bethany, and then kindly she added, 'that's how you measure a horse's height... in hands. A hand is four inches, or just over ten centimetres... so Rosie is about five foot three, or...' She waved a hand. 'I don't know how many centimetres! We still tend to measure horses the old-fashioned way.'

Katy, who is clever at maths, did a bit of silent calculation and with an air of triumph announced, 'One point six metres!'

I said, '*Wow.*'

'I'm impressed!' said Bethany.

I reached up and gently stroked Rosie's nose. 'Will we be able to ride her one day?' I asked.

Bethany said, 'One day. When you've grown a bit!

You could probably walk her round the field, once you've learnt the basics.'

I would have given anything to walk her round the field right there and then! I was quite disappointed when Bethany put her back in her stall and brought out two tiny little ponies for us – a stocky black one with a shaggy coat, and a chestnut, slightly taller, with a white star on her forehead.

Katy perked up immediately. 'Oh,' she said. 'That's better!'

'More your size,' nodded Bethany.

I pulled a bit of a face. The ponies were cute, especially the shaggy black one, which had a really cheeky face, but I would so have liked to show Bethany how cool I was. I'd have scrambled on to Rosie right away if only she'd have let me.

Bethany had obviously noticed my face-pulling. 'Don't you worry,' she said. 'One of these is a right little goer. He'll give you a run for your money!'

Eagerly I said, 'Which one?' I could almost feel Katy starting to quiver.

'Jet.' Bethany pointed to the little shaggy black one. He was standing there seemingly as good as gold, but I could see that he definitely had a naughty glint in his eye. 'He's not vicious,' Bethany assured us. 'He's actually quite a comedian. But he will take advantage, if you let him. Shetlands are notoriously self-willed! Strong too, although they're small. Freya, now –' she led the other pony forward – 'she'll do what she's told. Far better behaved, aren't you, my darling?' She put an arm round Freya's neck and hugged her. 'She's a good girl, this one! Okay, so who wants which?'

Katy looked at me pleadingly. I am taller than she is, so by right I should have been the one to have Freya. But Jet had that wicked glint in his eye! Freya was a lady. And she was pretty! Katy is pretty. Pretty with red-gold hair, whereas I have dark hair and my mum calls me sallow. My hair is dark and I don't *think* I could be called pretty. I certainly don't have a nice little round face like Katy. Funny little Jet was more my sort of horse! He might be short and stumpy and have great big hooves like dinner plates, but so what? He was a comedian, and sometimes so am I!

'I'll have Jet,' I said.

Katy was really grateful. And she looked so good mounted on Freya, both of them so elegant, almost like they had been made for each other, that I really didn't mind. Bethany told me she thought we'd made the right choices, as I seemed to have more confidence than Katy.

'You've obviously got a feel for it. You should do well.'

She didn't say it in front of Katy, and I didn't pass it on, even though I was bursting to do so! I couldn't resist telling Mum, though, when I got home.

'I knew I'd be good at riding! It's just something I felt.'

'Pity you didn't feel it about maths,' said Mum.

Now, why did she have to go and bring that up? Just when I was feeling so pleased with myself!

Trying not to sound cross, I said, 'I didn't feel it about maths because I'm not any good at maths!'

'Tell me about it,' said Mum.

I rolled my eyes. Me and maths was a bit of a sore subject. I'd got a D on our most recent test. Mrs Simmons had said it would have been a D– if the marks had gone that low. On last term's report she'd written, 'I don't believe Hannah is anywhere near as useless as she makes out. A bit more application would work wonders.' Huh! That was all she knew. Just as there are some people that can't understand letters, so there are some that can't understand numbers. And I am one of them! Nothing to do with application.

For our first few lessons me and Katy had to stay in the indoor ring, just learning how to hold the reins and how to sit properly – straight-backed, elbows tucked into our sides, heels down.

'Down, down! Heels *down!*' Bethany kept shouting it, as we slowly plodded round the ring.

'I can't!' wailed Katy. 'My *toes* keep going down!'

'Well, don't let them! Just keep saying to yourself… *heels, heels… heels down!*'

'They still won't go!' Katy was beginning to sound desperate. 'I think there's something wrong with my feet!'

'Rubbish!' said Bethany. 'Your feet are perfectly normal. Watch Hannah… see how she does it!'

'Heels *down*!' I chanted to Katy, as we collected our bikes at the end of the lesson.

'It's no good,' moaned Katy. 'I'm never going to get the hang of it!'

'You will!' I said. I said it quite fiercely. I didn't want to go riding on my own! Best friends do things together. 'You can't give up,' I said. 'Not if you're going to be a vet!' Katy was going to be a vet; I was going to run an animal sanctuary. We had it all planned. 'You can't be a vet if you don't know about horses!'

'I could still know about them,' muttered Katy. And then, before I had a chance to start arguing with her, she said, 'Let's go and look round the shopping centre!'

I pulled a face. I wasn't really in the mood for looking round the shopping centre. I had this pony book I'd got from the library and was dying to get back to it, but Katy was obviously keen so I said okay, if she really wanted to. I suppose, to be honest, I felt a bit guilty, what with Bethany holding me up as an example and poor Katy struggling.

When we reached the centre, carefully padlocking our bikes to the railings, we found there was a table parked just inside the entrance with a big banner above it saying **ANIMAL SAMARITANS**. Behind the table there was an elderly lady wearing a bright yellow tabard with the same words printed on it. Needless to say, we couldn't resist going up to have a look. Anything to do with animals and we are right there!

The lady asked us if we felt like signing her petition against the fur trade. Both me and Katy think killing animals for their fur is really cruel, so naturally we signed straight away. Then we noticed that on her table the lady had a tray full of badges, also saying *Animal Samaritans*, and all with cute pictures of various different animals. I asked if I could have one and the lady said

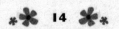

yes, so long as I was prepared to swear that I would 'help animals in need whenever and wherever I could'. Very solemnly I said, 'I swear', and Katy said that she did too, so the lady gave us each a card, saying that we were now officially Animal Samaritans and could choose badges for ourselves. I chose a dog, a dog being what I wanted more than anything else in the world, and Katy chose a cat, as she lived in hope of being able to talk her mum (who is rather house-proud) into letting her have one. We promised that we would wear our badges everywhere! It was important, said Katy, as we fetched our bikes, that everyone should know what we stood for.

'Cos then if they hear about an animal that needs help, like being abandoned or ill treated they'll know they can come to us and we'll do something about it.'

I said, 'Absolutely!'

I almost couldn't wait. I wanted to start rescuing animals right there and then!

*

When I got home and excitedly told Mum, thinking she would be pleased to have a daughter that cared about stuff other than boys and clothes and computer games, all of which she is constantly grumbling about, she just frowned and said, 'When you say *do something*... what sort of something are you talking about?'

I said we couldn't really tell until the time came, just that we would be prepared to go anywhere and do anything if it meant helping an animal in trouble. Mum made a little grunting noise, like 'Hm!'

'I thought you'd be happy,' I said. 'Don't you *like* me caring about animals?'

Mum said of course she did, but she hoped I wasn't getting myself mixed up with a group of people that used violence, or broke the law.

I said, 'Breaking the law how?'

'Well, like smashing shop windows or breaking into laboratories,' said Mum.

I assured her that Animal Samaritans wasn't like that. We had heard the elderly lady (whose name was Pat) arguing quite fiercely with a boy who belonged to a group called Direct Action. She had said that violence was not the way forward. I didn't tell Mum that while I wouldn't, of course, be *violent*, I would quite happily break the law if it meant rescuing an animal that was in distress – well, I would if I was brave enough, which I would like to think that I was. To be honest, I'm not really sure. I do sometimes have these dreams of running into burning buildings and snatching poor terrified animals from the jaws of death, or creeping out over frozen lakes, with the ice cracking ominously beneath me, to pluck a drowning dog to safety, but since I have so far not actually been put to the test it is difficult to say for certain. One thing I did know was that it would be asking for trouble to say anything to Mum!

One Sunday, when Katy and I went for our riding lesson, Bethany said she thought the time had come for us to try going on a real ride. Or a hack, as she called it. I

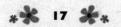

was a bit puzzled by this as I thought hacking was what people did when they broke into other people's computers and caused problems, but it seemed that in the horsey world it just meant going for a ride. Needless to say, I was thrilled!

'Don't get too excited,' warned Bethany. 'It's just a gentle stroll… maybe a bit of trotting. We'll see how you go.'

'Do you really think we're ready for it?' quavered Katy.

'Absolutely! You can't stay stuck in the ring forever; you'll get bored, and so will the horses. Now, take these.'

She held out a couple of hard hats. Katy looked at them doubtfully.

'Are these in case we fall off?'

'You are not going to fall off,' said Bethany. 'It's just the law, that's all.'

Someone suddenly called out to us from one of the stalls. 'I don't know what you're panicking for. A baby couldn't fall off Freya; she only ever goes anywhere at the walk.'

We froze. We knew that loud, clanging voice! It belonged to Tara Wilkinson, a particularly obnoxious girl in our class at school. Katy and I called her Motormouth, because that was what she was: all gobby and gabby and full of herself. One of those people that has opinions on everything under the sun.

'This is Tara,' said Bethany. 'I think you know one another, don't you? She's going to be joining us on the ride.'

My heart went *thunk*, right down to my boots, which, in fact, weren't boots at all but just ordinary shoes. Our mums had said they weren't going to fork out for expensive riding gear until we'd been doing it long enough to be quite sure that we wanted to go on doing it. So in the meantime we had to wear shoes and jeans and anoraks, and borrow hard hats from the ones that were kept at the stables.

It was very belittling, especially when we looked at

Motormouth in her smart tweedy jacket and her stretchy riding trousers and her long shiny boots. *And* she had a superior blue velvet hat. The stable hats were just ordinary black ones, all battered and bashed.

'You really ought to get hats of your own,' she told us. 'It's not very hygienic wearing commonal ones.'

Crushingly I said, 'I take it you mean *communal*?'

'Ones that other people have worn,' said Motormouth, growing all crimson and angry. She just hates it when someone gets the better of her!

Bethany led us away to help saddle up our horses. We'd had a bit of practice but I still found putting the bridle on a bit of a mystery. Katy, on the other hand, had no trouble at all, which obviously pleased her. We'd both been shown how to tighten the girth once we were actually mounted, so that the saddle would be secure and not start slipping sideways. I had worried in case I might tighten it too much and make poor Jet uncomfortable, but Bethany assured me that wouldn't happen.

'He's up to all the tricks,' she said. 'He knows how to puff himself out so you're fooled into thinking it's tight enough.'

It worried me when she said that. I wondered if it meant he didn't like having his saddle put on.

'Maybe it makes him uncomfortable?'

'Now, I ask you,' said Bethany, 'does he look like a horse that's uncomfortable?'

I had to say that he didn't. He was a really cheeky little fellow! Today especially, his eyes were bright, his ears well forward.

'That,' said Bethany, 'is a horse that's eager to go!'

I was eager too. Our first real ride! Needless to say, old Motormouth had her own pony, which she kept at the stables. She was called Caramel and just oozed quality. Beautiful and golden, with a creamy mane and tail. A palomino, the Mouth self-importantly informed us.

'Daddy bought her for my birthday. She was massively expensive!'

You can see why Motormouth is not one of our

favourite people. I mean, anyone who can boast that their pony is worth a lot of money! If I had a pony, I wouldn't care what it was worth. I wouldn't care if it wasn't worth anything at all. I would still love it and take care of it. And I would never, *ever* sell it on. I hate the way people do that! *Oh*, they say, *I've grown out of this pony, I need something bigger, I need something better.* If I was ever lucky enough to have a pony of my own, it would be for LIFE.

Unless, perhaps, it went to a sanctuary – say, if I ran out of money and could no longer afford to look after it. But not just to sell it on, when for all you knew it could end up as horsemeat.

I wasn't thinking of horsemeat, that day I went for my first ride. I was too busy being happy! There were just the four of us, me and Katy, Bethany and Motormouth. Bethany was riding Rosie. I'd never seen Rosie out before. She was the most beautiful, beautiful horse! Shiny, like satin, and really intelligent. Bethany said she only had to touch her and she would respond.

'I almost only have to *think*.'

'That's what you can do with a good horse,' said Motormouth. And she turned and stared disdainfully at me and Katy on Jet and Freya. I felt quite insulted on Jet's behalf! I'd become really fond of that funny chunky little pony.

'Jet will do anything I ask him,' I said. I was only saying it because she made me so angry! I honestly didn't have any idea if he would do what I asked. Going for a ride is very different from just being in the ring with Bethany shouting encouragement, but I touched him with my heels, the way we'd been taught, and sure enough he broke into a trot!

I said, 'Good boy, Jet! Good boy!' and he tossed his shaggy head and stepped out ever so proudly. Up-down, up-down, up-down. And me going up-down with him! Rising to the trot was what Bethany said it was called. It was the most incredible and amazing feeling.

If you *don't* rise to the trot, it is hugely uncomfortable. Get the timing wrong so that the horse is going up-down while you are going down-up – well! That is a recipe for disaster. At the very least it will give you a sore bum.

That was what was happening to poor old Katy. She just couldn't get the rhythm right! I saw her bouncing about on top of the saddle, and I felt for her, I really did, but I was just so… excited! I squeezed with my thighs and urged Jet to trot even faster, trit-trot, trit-trot, his little stumpy legs smashing up and down, with Motormouth's palomino swishing her tail in his face as we moved up the lane.

Bethany glanced back to see how we were all getting on. 'Everyone okay?'

'Why wouldn't we be?' muttered Motormouth.

'Katy? Hannah? Okay?'

I assured her that I was.

'Katy? How about you? You managing?'

Katy called back, 'Just about!', which I thought was really brave of her considering she was still bouncing up and down like a pea on top of a fountain.

At the end of the lane we came to a stretch of land

that is known to local horse riders as the Gallops, where, if you are experienced, you can go flat out.

'Can we gallop, can we gallop?' demanded Motormouth. 'Let's go!'

'*No*.' Bethany caught hold of Caramel's bridle. 'Katy and Hannah aren't ready for that.'

'I could gallop,' I said.

I can see now that it was really selfish of me. I was just showing off in front of Motormouth; I wasn't even considering poor Katy. Fortunately Bethany stood firm. She said there would be *no galloping* on this ride.

Needless to say, the Mouth fell into the most tremendous sulk and started grumbling about having to come out with beginners.

'You didn't have to come if you didn't want to,' said Bethany. 'You know perfectly well they've only just started riding. And anyway, Rosie can't gallop. You just fall in behind me and hold that horse back. We may do a bit of gentle cantering later on, when we get to the field. But only if I say!'

The Mouth muttered, but did as she was told. She reined in next to me and mumbled something about horses not being much good if they couldn't do what was expected of them.

'Are you talking about Rosie?' I said. I'd thought it odd when Bethany said she couldn't gallop. A big beautiful horse like that!

Motormouth thwacked sullenly at Caramel's neck with the reins. 'Ought to be pensioned off.'

'Why?' I said. 'Is she old?'

'No, but her lungs are shot. She's no use any more. You can't keep a horse that's no use!'

'You mean...' I wasn't quite sure that I understood. When she said that Rosie's lungs were shot —

'She's broken-winded!' Motormouth snapped it at me irritably. 'It means she can't breathe properly. That's why she can't gallop. It's like when people have asthma.'

'Oh!' I stared in dismay. 'Oh, poor Rosie! How did she get it?'

'She was in a fire. Only no one told the stupid person

that bought her and he didn't bother getting her checked out, so she was just a *total* waste of money. Which is why the owner's done a bunk and Mrs Foster's stuck with a horse she can't use.'

Mrs Foster was the woman who ran the stables. She barked a lot, and was rather stern and hatchet-faced. I was always glad it was Bethany who was teaching us to ride and not her! She would have freaked Katy out completely.

'You mean…' I was struggling to make sense of things. 'The owner just abandoned her?'

'Yes.'

'You mean, like… he just brought her in one day and left her?'

The Mouth heaved an impatient sigh. 'She was here as a livery. Like Caramel. Okay?'

I nodded doubtfully. I didn't like to ask what a livri was, but old Motormouth guessed I had no idea. She gave me this withering glance. I could tell she was thinking, *These non-horsey people, they are just so ignorant!*

But there was no call for her to be all superior. Everyone has to learn.

'It means –' she flapped a hand impatiently – 'board and lodging. The stables look after the horse and feed it and the owner pays them. So naturally, once this stupid person discovered he'd bought a knackered horse, he did a bunk. Just ran off and left her.'

'That's terrible!' I said.

'Yeah, Mrs Foster wasn't very pleased, stuck with a horse she can't use. Can't even sell her on; she's not worth anything. She does nothing but eat and cost money.'

'Won't her lungs get any better?' I said.

'No, I told you, they're completely shot.'

I didn't ask her what she meant by shot. I guessed she meant that, alas, they had been ruined for all time.

'She's so beautiful!' I said.

'Yeah, and she just stands about all day, eating her head off. All she's good for is going on beginner rides. Honestly, this is just *so* frustrating!'

She slapped at Caramel with the reins. Caramel

twitched and jumped. I could tell she was just longing to go.

'We usually fly along this bit!'

'It's not Rosie's fault,' I said.

'I know it's not her *fault*. But she really ought to be pensioned off. Either that, or—'

I didn't hear the next bit, which was probably just as well. It was almost certainly something horrible. The Mouth really was *the* most unfeeling person. She went whisking off, all full of herself, to join Bethany at the front. I was left to struggle with Jet, who was impatiently tossing his head up and down, desperate to go after her. By hauling as hard as I could on the reins I just about managed to hold him back. I worried afterwards that it wasn't very kind to haul on a horse's reins, but when I mentioned it to Bethany she said that Jet was known for getting the bit between his teeth and it wouldn't actually have hurt him. He probably hadn't even noticed.

'Shetlands are feisty little creatures.'

All the same, I thought, I wouldn't do it again. Not unless I absolutely had to.

Katy, as she caught me up, said, 'Are you having trouble?'

'Not really,' I said. 'It's just that stupid Motormouth, showing off. I was all right until then.'

'Trust her,' said Katy.

I said, 'Yes, she's totally unfeeling. All she cares about is whether a horse can earn money. She said poor Rosie is useless and ought to be pensioned off!'

'Why?' said Katy.

'Because she can't earn her keep.'

I explained about Rosie's lungs and how she couldn't gallop, and Katy said, 'I don't see that it matters so long as she can still walk and trot. I mean, who *wants* to gallop, anyway?'

She agreed with me, though, that it was terrible for such a big, beautiful horse to be so handicapped and that Motormouth was unspeakably loathsome. I said that I wouldn't mind *quite* so much if by pensioned off she meant Rosie being allowed to live out the rest of her days in a big grassy field with lots of other horses for company.

'But I have this feeling –' I said it darkly – 'that she meant something quite different.'

Katy looked alarmed. 'Like what?'

I shook my head. 'I don't want to think about it!'

Bethany and Motormouth were waiting for us at the end of the Gallops.

'Good girl!' Bethany nodded approval at me. 'You managed to hold him back. No thanks to you,' she added, giving the Mouth a bit of a black look. 'You were supposed to stay at the rear.'

Motormouth said sullenly that Caramel was getting frustrated. 'She wants to go!'

'Well, she's not going to go. You just keep her under control! You knew it was only going to be a gentle hack.'

We turned off the Gallops into Stiles Farm Lane, where Bethany said that we could now do a little bit of cantering.

'But only if you're feeling up to it. Katy? You want to give it a go?'

Katy very bravely said okay. As for me, I couldn't wait!

'Tara? Just a canter. All right?'

Old Motormouth pulled a face and said she supposed so, but even a canter wasn't enough to satisfy her. We'd hardly hit the lane before she and Caramel went careering off. Rosie pranced a bit, but Bethany very firmly held her back. I *tried* to hold Jet, but he was just too strong. He lit out after Caramel as if a whole herd of tigers were behind us. I really thought I was going to come off! Somehow or other I managed to hang on, even though I half slipped out of the saddle and ended up losing the reins and clutching in panic at his mane. It was actually quite frightening, because what if he never stopped? What if he just went hurtling out of the lane and into a stream of traffic? I was never so relieved as when he pulled up, snorting, beside Motormouth and Caramel.

Bethany was absolutely furious. She gave the Mouth

this long lecture on BAD MANNERS and LACK OF CONSIDERATION.

'If Hannah had broken her neck, it would have been all your fault!'

Good little Freya had behaved perfectly, which was just as well as Katy told me afterwards that she would have been terrified.

'Weren't *you* terrified?' she said. 'Just a little bit?'

'No way,' I told her. 'It was exciting!'

Well, I didn't want to put her off. No point admitting I'd nearly had a heart attack!

When we got back to the stables we put our ponies away and removed their tack (another new word – the horsey term for the saddle and bridle), then gave them their carrots, kissed them goodbye and rushed off to say hello to Rosie. Although we loved Jet and Freya, Rosie was our favourite. She was everyone's favourite! A great big spoilt darling.

'And so she ought to be,' said Katy.

She was so kind, and sweet, and gentle. One time

when I was helping muck out (cleaning her stable!) she went and stood on my foot with one of her great slab-like hooves. Some horses, if they do that, will just go on standing there while your foot slowly *c-r-u-n-c-h-e-s* beneath their weight. Really painful! You have to shove at them to get them off. But Rosie realised immediately what she'd done. I didn't even have to yell. I just made this little 'oof!' sound, but she'd already lifted her hoof and moved it away. And she never, ever bit or kicked or tried to crush you against the side of the stall, which is what some horses can do if they're feeling a bit mean. We always went to say goodbye to her and give her something special, like a nice juicy apple.

Bethany was still with her. She'd hung her saddle over the door and was rubbing her down.

'Why is she all wet?' asked Katy.

Bethany said that she'd sweated a bit. 'It's not good to leave them like that.'

'The others didn't sweat,' I said. It wasn't a specially warm day and the ride – which Motormouth was still muttering about – had only been a beginners' one, not a mad dash about the countryside. 'Is it because of her lungs?'

'I'm afraid so.' Bethany blew softly up Rosie's nostrils. She had told us that horses like you to do that; it was a way of communicating with them. Sometimes they blew back, lovely soft horsey breath smelling of grass and hay. 'You have to be taken care of, don't you, my big gentle girl?'

'But so long as she's looked after –' Katy said it anxiously – 'she'll be all right?'

'Well… yes.' Bethany didn't sound terribly certain.

'She won't get any *worse*?' I said.

'Not if she's treated properly. She really needs to retire. She needs to live in a meadow! She shouldn't have to go on working. She's been through such a lot! Can you imagine how it must feel to be a horse, shut up in a box, with fire raging all about you? It must have been absolutely terrifying for her.'

Katy stroked Rosie's neck. I reached up and put my

finger in her big rubbery lip and wobbled it about. For some reason she seemed to enjoy it when I did that.

'What will happen to her?' said Katy.

'I don't know.' Bethany snatched the saddle off the top of the door. 'Don't ask me. I don't want to think about it!'

That was all she would say. She wouldn't talk to us any more.

Worriedly we walked across to the caravan, which was where Mrs Foster had her office, to pay for our ride. I suppose we could have asked Mrs Foster what was going to happen to Rosie, but she was such a cold, unwelcoming sort of person that we didn't like to. It was Motormouth who told us. She came running out to join us as we went to fetch our bikes.

'Bethany doesn't like talking about Rosie. It upsets her.'

'Well, it *is* upsetting,' I said. I said it quite fiercely. She'd better not start on again about how Rosie wasn't earning her keep!

The Mouth said, 'Yeah, but she's just heard what's going to happen.'

'What?' said Katy. 'What's going to happen?'

'She's going to the knacker's,' said Motormouth. 'Going to be turned into horsemeat.'

CHAPTER 2

Katy and me couldn't believe it! We thought it was a joke. A sick, horrible kind of joke. Certainly not the sort that any normal human being would make, but Motormouth is a sick, horrible kind of person. She goes fox hunting and thinks it's all right for people to wear fur and club baby seals to death. She is truly disgusting!

'Ask Mrs Foster if you don't believe me,' she said. 'She'll tell you. She's sending her for horsemeat.'

The way she said it made me go cold. That big, soft, gentle girl was going to have her life taken from her, and Motormouth couldn't have cared less.

Horsey people can sometimes be very hard. I have noticed this.

'It's no use crying over what can't be helped,' said Motormouth. 'It's how they'll all end up, probably.'

'*What?*' We stared at her, horrified.

'All of them.' She flapped a hand towards the stables. 'When they can't be used any more. What else do you do with them?'

'You keep them!' I said.

Katy didn't say anything. I think for once she was truly at a loss for words.

The Mouth was looking at me disdainfully. She said, 'Keep them *where*, exactly?'

I said, 'In a field!'

'Doing what? Eating their heads off?'

'Not doing anything! Just enjoying their retirement.'

Katy suddenly found her tongue. 'Old people retire! Why can't horses?'

'Some do,' said Motormouth. 'If their owners can afford it. But obviously you can't if you're running a business.'

Motormouth's dad is a farmer and so she is used to

innocent animals being dragged off to the slaughterhouse. She doesn't see anything wrong in it. She thinks people like me and Katy are just stupid and sentimental.

'You have to be realistic,' she said. 'That's your trouble! You're just *so* sentimental. At the end of the day animals are only animals.'

What was that supposed to mean, *at the end of the day*?

'They still have feelings,' I said.

'Not like we do. Anyway, we're the top species.'

It was what she'd said to us when we'd announced that we had become vegetarians: *we're the top species.* Meaning it was okay to stuff yourself with chunks of dead animal.

Angrily Katy said, 'Being top species doesn't mean we have to go around killing everything!'

'No,' I said. 'It means we have a duty to look after them.'

'We do look after them, while they're alive,' said Motormouth.

'Well, you couldn't very well look after them when they're dead!' I retorted.

'I didn't mean that!' Old Motormouth had gone all red and blotchy. She always goes red when she tries arguing with me and Katy. It's because she can't ever get the better of us. Cruelty is cruelty, and that's all there is to it.

'What I *meant*,' she said, 'is that the horse is a working animal. You can't afford to go on feeding them if they're not earning any money. It's just not practical.'

Which was something, I bet, she'd got from her dad.

In heated tones Katy said, 'Horses weren't put on this earth to earn money for human beings!'

'How do you know?' said Motormouth. It's the sort of childish argument she always resorts to. 'How does anyone know what any of us were put here for? All we can say for sure is that we're at the top of the chain!'

'If we're that superior,' said Katy, 'it seems to me we ought to be taking care of other species, not just using them to make money and then murdering them when they're too old.'

'Or too sick,' I added. I always do my best to support Katy whenever I can, though I am not as clever at arguing as she is.

'There ought to be a law against it,' I said. 'Everybody that owns a horse should be made to sign something saying they'll let it retire when it can't work any more.'

'Yesss!' Katy, triumphant, punched the air with her clenched fist. 'A pension fund for horses!'

'Like for human beings.'

'And rest homes—'

'Rest fields—'

'Where they could all live together and be happy and just amble about doing their own thing.'

'That is what *ought* to happen,' I said.

'Oh, get real!' snapped the Mouth. 'Stupid townies!'

She calls us that because she has always lived in the country and thinks herself superior. She will probably still be saying it when we are old and wizened and

haven't set foot in a town for nigh on fifty years. *If* we're still on speaking terms, which most probably we won't be. With any luck a herd of maddened cows will have run her over and crushed her long before that.

A big flash car had pulled up in the yard. The Mouth went stalking over to it.

'Good riddance,' muttered Katy.

'Do you think –' I stood, undecided, astride my bike – 'do you think it's true what she said? About Rosie?'

There was a silence. I thought for a moment that Katy wasn't going to say anything, but then she burst out, 'It's so unfair! It's not her fault she can't earn money. She can't help being sick!'

I said, 'No, it was human beings that did it to her.'

'And now they're going to kill her!'

I drew a long, quivering breath. 'I suppose, really, we ought to go and ask Mrs Foster.'

We most desperately didn't want to. I mean, for one thing we were a bit scared of her. We'd once heard her being really nasty to a woman who had fallen off her horse while out on a ride and hadn't managed to hang on to the reins, so that her horse had gone galloping off. She had reduced that poor woman to tears. But then, also, there was the other thing: as long as we didn't hear it *officially* we could go on pretending that the Mouth had just been making up stories to alarm us.

'You know what she's like,' I said.

Katy agreed that we did. She said that Motormouth was vile and evil and you couldn't necessarily believe a word she said. But she still thought we ought to do it.

I sighed deeply. I knew she was right. If you have sworn to be an Animal Samaritan, you can't just close your eyes and make like something isn't happening.

We propped our bikes against the side of the tack room and trailed back into the stables. Mrs Foster was in her office caravan. She was adding things up on a calculator. Probably working out how much all her horses were earning before she sent them off to be murdered.

I suddenly came over all bold and defiant and rapped

quite smartly at the door. We were Animal Samaritans! Nobody scared us!

Mrs Foster looked up and scowled. She was always scowling. It just seemed like it was her natural expression.

'Yes,' she said. 'Katy and Hannah… What can I do for you?'

The words came blurting out of me: 'We want to know if it's true about Rosie!'

It probably didn't sound very polite, but I wasn't feeling polite. We had sworn to defend animals!

Mrs Foster, all icy, said, 'Is what true?'

'That she's –' I lowered my voice to a whisper – 'that she's going to be turned into horsemeat?'

It seemed truly terrible to be saying such a thing in a stable full of horses. They are such intelligent creatures! They might not be able to understand *everything* that is said, but they can certainly pick up on feelings. Suppose Rosie had heard her name and pricked her ears forward to listen?

I could see that Mrs Foster didn't like being questioned.

She probably considered it an impertinence, because who were me and Katy? Just two stupid townies who'd lived most of their lives in London and didn't understand the ways of the countryside.

'I accept that it's not pleasant,' she said. 'None of us enjoy it, but we do not live in a perfect world and I am not a charity. I have a business to run. She's not my horse, I didn't want her, I'm just the poor fool who's left to pick up the tab.'

Whatever a tab was. The bill, I *think* she meant.

Katy, very fiercely, said, 'It's not Rosie's fault!'

Surely even a hatchet-faced woman like Mrs Foster had to have *some* feelings?

Hatchet Face twitched angrily.

'For your information,' she said, 'I have been paying for that horse's food and keep for the past three months. I cannot go on indefinitely. If the person who bought her had had the elementary common sense to get her checked out by a vet before parting with his money…' She paused. 'Well! The horse would no doubt have gone to the knacker's there and then, or worse still been sent abroad to be slaughtered, so at least it's had a few more months of life. Now, if you'll excuse me, I'm busy.'

With that, she wrenched open her desk drawer, tossed the calculator in and slammed the drawer shut so hard I was surprised it didn't shatter. She was in a *really* bad mood.

Katy and I walked miserably away. Our footsteps carried us round to the other side of the indoor ring, to Rosie's box. Her big horsey head was hanging over the door. I put my finger in her lower lip and wobbled it, the way she liked.

Katy was struggling with tears. 'She has no idea!'

That set me off as well. I felt the tears come welling up. It is terrible the way that animals place their trust in human beings, only to be let down. To be herded into wagons and driven to their deaths. To be locked in cages and tortured. To be clubbed and shot and brutally butchered. I think wild creatures are sensible to keep away from us. I know I would!

Bethany could obviously see that we were upset. She came over to us and said, 'I suppose you've heard the bad news about Rosie?'

I nodded. I couldn't trust myself to actually speak.

'It's horrid, I know,' said Bethany, 'but it's not Pippa's fault.' Pippa was Mrs Foster. Honestly! She didn't look in the least like a Pippa. More like a… a *Gertrude* or a *Helga*. Something mean and pinched and hard.

'It's the owner,' said Bethany. 'Just walking off and dumping her on us! He's the one to blame. You don't think Pippa *likes* having to send a horse to the knacker's yard?'

'Then why do it?' sobbed Katy.

'She's been trying not to. She's kept putting it off. But sooner or later she has to call it a day. She's running a stables, not a sanctuary.'

'But it's so cruel!' I said.

'It's life,' said Bethany sadly.

'You mean *death*!' shouted Katy.

We just couldn't accept it. We had become Animal

Samaritans to fight for all those poor defenceless creatures who weren't able to fight for themselves. We couldn't let poor Rosie go for horsemeat!

On the way home we met one of our neighbours, old Mrs B. We always called her old Mrs B. It may sound a bit rude – even a bit ageist – but she is forever telling us how ancient she is and that that is why she can't understand computers or even cope with a smartphone.

'Too newfangled for the likes of me!'

Maybe when I get to be her age – she is eighty-seven! – I will be doing the same thing.

'Too newfangled for the likes of me,' I will say, as all the young people go round plugged directly into the internet, half human and half cyborg. I'm not sure I like the sound of it even now! I don't think you could have the same feelings for animals if you were only half human.

Mrs B is always incredibly cheerful in spite of being eighty-seven and having to walk with a stick. She has this very sweet old Staffie called Sidney. Some people

are scared of Staffies (otherwise known as Staffordshire bull terriers). They think they are vicious and should all be muzzled. It's just not true! They are one of the *very best breeds* to have around children. Sidney, in particular, is one big softie. He came wobbling up to us, his old tail slowly wagging from side to side, looking for his usual cuddle.

'Dear me,' said Mrs B. 'You two are looking a bit plum duff!'

I did my best to smile, but I could feel my mouth starting to wobble. Katy, bravely, said, 'What's plum duff?'

'Plum duff, rough?' Mrs B was born in London, within the sound of Bow Bells, which meant she was a true Cockney and knew lots of Cockney rhyming slang. Katy and I had managed to learn a little bit. *Tea leaf*, for example, meaning *thief*, and *apples and pears* for *stairs*. *Plum duff* was a new one!

'So, come on,' said Mrs B. 'You can tell an old lady… What's happened to upset you? Trouble at school?'

I sighed. Katy plucked at her handkerchief.

'Trouble at school,' she said, 'would be *nothing*.'

'Oh.' Mrs B slowly nodded. 'It'll be to do with animals, then?'

She knew all about us and our feelings for animals. She'd already helped us rescue a pigeon that we'd found with a damaged wing, and just last week had let us go into her back garden to make a little tunnel under the fence for the hedgehogs to use. She was such a lovely old lady! Our mums both have this tendency to groan when we do what they call *starting on*.

'Oh,' they go, 'not that again?'

They are glad we are not obsessed with boys or clothes or make-up, but they do sometimes get a bit tired of our great passion for animals. Mrs B is always sympathetic.

'So, come on,' she said. 'Out with it!'

I took a deep quivering breath. 'There's this girl,' I said, 'that's in our class and goes riding at the same stables, and she said – she said…'

I stopped, unable to go on. Katy took up the story: 'She said that most horses that are in riding schools end up as horsemeat!'

Gravely Mrs B said that she was probably right. 'It's one of the hard facts of life, I'm afraid. With the best will in the world, you can't rescue them all.'

Katy blotted rather fiercely at her eyes. 'Just because we can't rescue them all doesn't mean we shouldn't try to rescue any!'

'Do I take it it's one horse in particular you're worried about?'

'Rosie!' I almost choked as I said it. 'She's the sweetest, dearest horse that wouldn't hurt a fly, but she can't earn her keep any more and we just don't know what to do!'

'Hm.' Mrs B thought about it for a moment. 'How about asking your friend Meg? At the sanctuary? See if she can suggest anything.'

Meg Hennessy is one of our favourite people. She runs a sanctuary called End of the Road, where sometimes we help out. But it is mainly for cats and dogs, and smaller animals such as rabbits and hedgehogs. Sadly I said, 'I don't think she'd have room for a horse.'

Mrs B said, 'No, but she might know someone who has. Give her a go! Why not?'

Mrs B and Sidney went on their way, towards the woods. Katy and I looked at each other.

'We're always asking Meg,' I said.

It was Meg we'd gone to with our damaged pigeon. We'd also gone to her with a baby hedgehog that we'd found in the road, and a frog that had dried out and that we had hoped she could bring back to life. Sadly she hadn't been able to, though she'd taken both the hedgehog and the pigeon. She'd explained that she wasn't really there for wildlife but she had friends that were.

Some people would have just sent us away, or impatiently given us telephone numbers and told us to go and find out for ourselves. Meg wasn't like that! She cared too much. It was why she was always rushed off her feet and why the sanctuary was always full to bursting. But Katy and I cared too! It wasn't like we'd be bothering her for selfish reasons.

'It is for *animals*,' said Katy.

'For Rosie,' I said.

That decided us. 'Let's do it!' said Katy.

We had to race home first to tell our mums, otherwise they would have started to flap and wring their hands and say, 'Where can they have got to?' And then they would think we had fallen off our bikes and broken our necks, which is the sort of thing that mums always seem to think you are doing. I suppose mums just can't help themselves. Their lives are one big worry!

I told Mum that we were going to the sanctuary to see Meg, but I didn't think it quite necessary to explain why. She would only have started on about not making a nuisance of ourselves. Fortunately she was in the middle of a rush job, which is what she calls a translation that has to be done in a simply stupendous hurry. All she said was, 'Don't be too long, I want you to keep an eye on Benjy for me while I get on with this wretched translation. If I don't finish it by this evening, I shall be in trouble!'

I told her no problem, and went racing back out. (Benjy is my little brother. My *annoying* little brother. Maybe all six-year-olds are annoying, but anyway it is part of what my pocket money is for, me keeping an eye on Benjy while Mum gets on with her rush jobs. I guess I don't really mind.)

Katy was waiting impatiently for me at the gate. We whizzed along to End of the Road in record time, only to discover that Meg wasn't there. Deirdre, who is her assistant, said that she had gone on a sponsored walk all the way to Wales to try and raise some money.

'Funds are really low. We're getting desperate.'

Our hearts plummeted when she said that. We both dug into our pockets to see if we had any money on us. Katy proudly produced a 50p piece and held it out. I could only find a twenty, but Deirdre said anything, no matter how small, was gratefully accepted.

'So what can I do for you?'

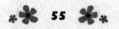

'Nothing, I don't expect.' I said it glumly.

'We wondered if you'd have room for a poor sick horse,' said Katy.

Deirdre sucked in her breath. 'Sorry, girls, but not a chance! We can barely feed the ones we've got. Unless, maybe, it's a Shetland pony?'

I heaved a sigh and said no, it was a big, beautiful horse that was going to be turned into horsemeat if we couldn't find some way of rescuing her.

'There's a horse sanctuary over Spindle Down,' said Deirdre. 'Spindle Down Rescue… they might be able to help. I'll find their number for you. But look, while you're here, you wouldn't feel like exercising some of the dogs for us, would you?'

We can never resist an appeal to exercise the poor abandoned dogs at End of the Road. They are so lost! And so bewildered. Where have their people gone? When are they going to come back for them? Sometimes, sadly, their people have died and there is no one left to take care of their beloved pets. Other times, people have simply decided they can't be bothered having a dog any more so they bring them along to Meg and say, 'Either you take it or we have it put down.' Occasionally they have even been so cruel as to just dump them and drive off, leaving the poor dog alone and broken-hearted. Dogs are so trusting, and so loyal! And they ask so little. Just to be loved and looked after. I was still living in hope that one day soon Mum might give in and let me adopt one of them. It would be hard to choose just one out of so many, but as Katy had so wisely said, just because you can't rescue all of them doesn't mean you shouldn't do what you can.

We spent an hour in the field throwing a ball and running and chasing. By the time we arrived home Mum was in a bit of a frazzle, wondering where I had got to.

'I thought you were coming straight back?'

'We did a bit of helping out,' I said.

'I just wish you could do a bit of helping out here,' grumbled Mum. 'I can't keep an eye on your brother

and get on with my work *and* decide what we're going to have for dinner *and*—'

'Mum,' I cried, 'don't worry! I'm here now. I'll decide about dinner. I'll even *get* the dinner! *And* I'll keep an eye on Benjy. You just sit there nice and quietly and do your work. I've just got to make a quick telephone call. I won't be a minute!'

I had promised Katy that I would ring the Spindle Down Rescue people as soon as I got in. I'd hoped I could do it without Mum finding out, as she tends to get a bit fussed about our dedication to animals. She thinks we take it too much to heart and that it interferes with schoolwork. Unfortunately she came into the kitchen as I was making the call and I saw her eyebrows go shooting up. Not that she really heard much because all I got was an answerphone message saying to please ring back in the morning unless it was an emergency – which was the bit that Mum heard.

'*Well?*' she said. '*Is it?*'

I hesitated, then put the phone down. I didn't want

to put people's backs up. I muttered that it wasn't an emergency *yet.*

'But it will be, if nothing is done!'

Mum groaned. 'What is it this time?'

I told her about Rosie. She shook her head. 'Not again!' she said. 'I really can't bear it!'

'Bear what?' I said.

'All the heartache and the breast-beating and you and Katy in floods of tears and wanting me to keep turkeys in the kitchen and wombats in the garden, and—'

'Mum, I have *never* wanted you to keep a wombat in the garden,' I said. I wasn't even sure what a wombat was.

'You wanted me to keep a turkey in the kitchen,' said Mum.

'Only for one night.' It hadn't been much to ask, had it? A turkey in the kitchen for just *one night*? Some poor Christmas turkey that had managed to escape from a horrible turkey farm? We'd found him wandering at the end of the lane. What were we supposed to do?

Just leave him there? He *could* have stayed with us, if End of the Road hadn't taken him in.

'Wombats, turkeys, I don't care,' said Mum. 'I'm certainly not having a horse in the back garden.'

Sadly I told her that a garden our size would be far too small for a horse like Rosie.

'Good,' said Mum.

'It's not good!' I said. 'Her life is at stake!'

'Hannah, please don't,' said Mum. 'Life's a big enough struggle as it is. I really can't cope with anything more.'

I explained to Mum, as patiently as I could, that now that we were officially Animal Samaritans Katy and I were dedicated to helping animals in need *whenever and wherever*. You couldn't just turn it on and off like a tap: it was a lifetime's commitment. You had to be prepared for a bit of heartbreak.

Oh, but lying in bed that night, tossing and turning, I had more than just a *bit* of heartbreak. I had nightmares. I kept imagining that poor sweet girl being dragged away to the knacker's yard, terrified, not knowing what was happening, smelling all the blood and the fear… maybe even being put on a boat and taken off to France to be slaughtered over there. I knew about these things. I desperately hadn't wanted to, but if you have promised to devote your life to animals you cannot just close your eyes. Katy and I had both signed petitions. We'd seen pictures of the poor frightened horses, crammed into the dark holds of the cross-Channel ferries, sometimes without any water, sometimes in agony with broken legs. And then, at the end of the journey, horrible rough men pushing them and pulling them, shouting at them, hitting them, forcing them towards their death.

I tried desperately to stop dwelling on it, but the images were in my head, and I couldn't get rid of them. It got so bad I had to stuff a hanky in my mouth to stop myself from screaming. At midnight I grabbed my phone and texted Katy: *Are you asleep?* She texted me back: *No, I can't stop thinking about Rosie.* I told her that I couldn't stop thinking, either. We agreed that one of us must ring the sanctuary first thing in the morning. I said that I would do it, and there and then I made a vow: our sweet gentle horse was not going to end her days in pain and fear. Not if Katy and I had anything to do with it!

CHAPTER
3

Next day was Monday, and so of course we had to go to school. There is always *something* that has to be done. Something that gets in the way of the really important stuff. Such as, in this case, ringing the sanctuary. I did try, on my mobile, but it was too early in the day and there was the same answerphone message as before. I began to despair. They still wouldn't be there by the time I got to school, and once I reached school I'd have to hand my phone in to the office because they are really strict about people not having their phones in the classroom and I couldn't see Ms McMaster, who is the school secretary, letting me make a call before assembly. She is not the most sympathetic of people. I once told her – thinking she would be interested – that I had seen a dear little mouse scuttling about by the recycling bins. All I wanted was for her to give me my phone back for just a few minutes so that I could take a photo. She wasn't having any of it! Just told me to hurry along because the bell had rung.

Mum wasn't having any of it, either. She wanted to know what I was doing, messing about on my phone instead of getting off to school. I told her that I was just ringing the sanctuary and she said, 'Not at this hour of the morning! Look at the time… you'll be late for school.'

Late for school! What did late for school matter when Rosie's life was at stake?

I said this to Mum and she said, 'Hannah, we've had all this out before. Your schoolwork comes first. *After* school is the time for rescuing animals.'

Like there is a set time for it! Like between the hours of half past eight and half past four animals must manage as best they can.

I said, 'Mum, this is an emergency! *Please*, Mum! Let me just wait till someone's there.'

She wouldn't, of course. They have this absolute obsession about school. Like if you just miss five minutes of it your entire life will be a disaster.

'Come on, Hannah!' Mum gave me a little push in the direction of the door. 'Don't keep Katy waiting.'

Benjy, banging his spoon up and down in his cereal bowl, took up the cry. 'Don' keep Katy waiting! Don' keep Katy waiting!'

I told him to shut up and Mum said, '*Hannah…*'

'I don't suppose you could do it?' I said.

'Do what?'

'Ring the sanctuary! See if they could take Rosie!'

'Oh, for goodness' sake,' said Mum. 'As if I haven't got enough on my plate! Why can't the people at the stables do it, if they're so bothered?'

I'd never thought of that. Why *couldn't* they? I guessed because Mrs Foster didn't actually care, in spite of what Bethany said. She just wanted to get rid of poor Rosie the quickest way possible. But Bethany cared! Why couldn't she have rung the sanctuary?

I found it really depressing that not even Bethany was prepared to lift a finger to help that big gentle horse. I felt the tears spring to my eyes. Mum obviously saw how upset I was.

'All right, all right!' she said. 'I'll ring them for you. If it's going to set your mind at rest, I'll do it.'

'Oh, Mum! Thank you!' I rushed at her and hugged her. 'You know what you've got to say?'

'Tell me,' said Mum.

'You've got to say that there's this darling beautiful horse that's got damaged lungs because of being in a fire and if someone doesn't rescue her *immediately* she's going to the knacker's yard!'

'So you want them to come and take her away?'

'Yes.' I nodded.

'Leave it with me,' said Mum. 'I'll see what I can do. You just get off to school and try to stop worrying.'

I got off to school but I couldn't stop worrying. I said

to Katy, 'Why couldn't Bethany have rung the sanctuary?'

Katy agreed it was a puzzle. After all, Bethany loved Rosie as much as we did. She couldn't bear the thought of her going for horsemeat.

'People just seem to let things happen,' said Katy sadly. 'They just can't be bothered.'

Like Bethany. It had probably never even occurred to her to ring up a sanctuary. When horses couldn't earn their keep any more they were sent off to be slaughtered. It was just the way it was.

'I suppose,' said Katy, 'it takes a bit of an effort.'

I said, 'Tell me about it!' And then I added that that was all the more reason for people like us to be Animal Samaritans. 'Because we're *prepared* to make an effort.'

It was only our second week back at school after the summer holidays. Our new class teacher was Mr O'Sullivan, who all the girls were mad about. Well, all except me and Katy. We didn't have the time for that sort of thing.

'All this dribbling and drooling,' said Katy, 'when they could be out there rescuing animals!'

The Mouth and her best friend Caley Hooper were two of the main droolers. At break that morning they proudly showed everyone how they'd tattooed the letters *PO'S* on their arms in felt-tip pen. The P, they told us, stood for Paul, which apparently was Mr O'Sullivan's first name. I have no idea how they discovered that.

Caley loftily said, 'We have ways of finding out.'

Soppily went and asked him, I bet.

Please, sir, what does the P stand for, sir? Is it Peter, sir? Is it Patrick, sir? Oh, sir, please, sir, tell us what it stands for, sir!

They'd become almost hysterical about it. It seemed that Paul O'Sullivan was the name of some singer they were mad about.

'Coincidence or what?'

'*Paul O'Sullivan,*' swooned Motormouth.

'Never heard of him,' said Katy.

'Me neither,' I said.

The Mouth curled her lip. 'That's because all you ever think about is animals!'

'Yes, and we're thinking about one right now,' said Katy. 'About a poor horse with damaged lungs that people want to *murder*.'

'Oh, heavens!' Caley clapped her hands to her ears. 'They're off again!'

'They can't help it,' said the Mouth. 'They just won't face the hard reality.'

'But why only care about animals? Far worse things happen to human beings.'

'Human beings aren't murdered just because they're sick!' retorted Katy.

Of course they ignored that. They always ignore things when they haven't got an answer.

'Just think,' said the Mouth, 'of all those people that are starving.'

Like she cared!

'If you didn't waste all your time and energy on animals—'

'Not to mention *money*,' said Caley. She had seen us that day in the shopping centre, putting all our change into the Animal Samaritans collecting tin. 'If you didn't give all your money to animals, you could give it to Oxfam and help *people*.'

'Do you give all your money to Oxfam?' said Katy.

Oh, brilliant! That got them. Caley turned bright scarlet and Motormouth snapped, 'I do when I can!'

'You do when you *can*? That doesn't make any sense!' said Katy. 'You either *do* give all your money or you *don't* give all your money. And if you *don't* give all your money—'

'You might just as well shut up,' I said.

I get so sick of people telling me and Katy that we ought to be helping human beings instead of animals. Like human beings are *so* much more important. And anyway, all these people, what do they do? Nothing! They just have a go at me and Katy. It absolutely annoys me.

Which is why I told Caley and the Mouth they might

as well shut up, and why they told me to go boil myself and next thing I knew we'd all got into this great slanging match, with insults flying across the room and bouncing off the walls. Mr O'Sullivan walked right into the middle of it, just in time to hear Motormouth screaming 'Pig's bum, you abject *idiot*!', which I reckon served her right.

Mr O'Sullivan said, 'I'll pretend I didn't hear that,' and Motormouth turned red from head to foot like some kind of human pillar box. She even had her mouth open! I felt like posting my maths book in it.

I thought about Rosie all day long. I kept wondering if Mum had telephoned yet, and if so what the sanctuary had said. They might even have sent a horsebox and rescued her already!

'I'd hate not seeing her again,' I said, 'but I wouldn't mind so long as she was safe.'

'And we could always go and visit,' said Katy. 'Spindle Down isn't that far. We could get there on our bikes!'

All we wanted to do at the end of school was to go rushing home. Instead we had to stay on for a boring

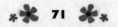

rehearsal for the end-of-term show. Well, that's not quite fair because it wasn't really boring. It was all about the Peasants' Revolt, which happened in 1351 and was led by a man called Wat Tyler, who was like the people's hero but was double-crossed by King Richard II and viciously murdered. Not having enough boys in the class meant that some of us – mostly the taller ones – had to be soldiers, while all the rest were peasants. Katy and I were peasants, which made the Mouth sneer but which we were glad about as we were both very firmly on the side of the people. If I had been around at the time, I would certainly have revolted! Motor-mouth, needless to say, sucked up to the king. *She* was playing the big bad captain, brutally riding people down with her horse.

Normally I enjoyed rehearsing, even though we had lots of songs to sing and I can't sing to save my life! Caley Hooper kept hissing, 'You're *flat!*' and screwing up her face like she was in agony. Ha! Maybe she was. Maybe my voice was my secret weapon. I could just go and *sing* into her ear whenever I wanted to annoy her. But I didn't really feel like singing that afternoon. I felt like racing home as fast as I could and finding out whether Rosie had been saved!

It was half past five before we got back. Katy had to go straight in for her tea, because her mum is really weird about mealtimes. If they don't happen when they're supposed to happen she goes a bit loopy; same if anyone treads mud across the kitchen floor or spills juice on to the carpet. You always have to be extra specially careful, like walking on eggshells.

Katy says she can't help it. 'She's a bit obsessive.'

Like we are about animals, except it seems to me that animals are worth being obsessed about, whereas who could possibly get worked up about a splodge of mud on the kitchen floor?

Katy called after me as I rushed off down the lane. 'Let me know what's happened!'

I reached our cottage, which is the last one in the row, and went tearing through the back door. Benjy

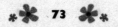

immediately hurled himself across the kitchen, going 'Hannah see, Hannah see!' and thrusting a sheet of drawing paper at me.

'Oh,' I said. 'A sausage with legs! How lovely.'

'Not a sossij! It's a *dog*.'

'A sausage dog!'

'Not a s—'

'Benjy, please, not now!' I said. Any other time I would have indulged him but I only had one thought in my mind at that moment. 'Mum?' I pushed past Benjy and went through into the hall. Mum was in the front room, at her desk. 'Mum, did you ring? What did they say? Are they going to take her?'

'Oh!' Mum sprang round. Her hand flew to her mouth. 'Oh, my goodness, Hannah! I'm so sorry! I clean forgot!'

'*Mum!*' I wailed. I couldn't believe it! She'd given me her *word*.

'Oh, Hannah, I'm sorry, I truly am! I tried them twice this morning and they were engaged both times, then the agency rang wanting to know if I'd finished this translation because it's needed really urgently, and I got into a panic and… I've been working ever since!'

I couldn't get mad at her. It's not very often that Mum lets me down. And she was so apologetic! She obviously felt bad about it. All the same it was a bitter blow.

'Try them now,' urged Mum. I did, but of course it was too late: I just got the answerphone again.

'I'll do it first thing tomorrow,' said Mum. 'I will, I promise!'

What could I say? That tomorrow might be too late?

Miserably I said that I had better ring Katy.

'Tell her,' said Mum, 'that I'm wearing sackcloth and ashes!'

Whatever that meant. I think it meant she was truly repentant. But what good was that if Rosie had already been sent off to meet her fate?

Katy came to the phone all bubbly and eager and full of hope. 'Hannah! What happened?'

I felt terrible having to break the news. If it had been Katy's mum who had let us down, I am not sure I would ever have been able to forgive her. I certainly wouldn't have behaved as well as Katy.

For a few seconds she didn't say anything, either because she was in the middle of eating her tea or because she didn't trust her voice not to give way. And then I heard a gulping sound, like she had a lump in her throat. And then she said, 'Oh.' And then, very bravely, 'I suppose it doesn't mean as much to your mum as it does to us. She doesn't know Rosie.'

'She's promised faithfully that she'll ring tomorrow,' I said.

'If Rosie's still alive!'

'Oh, don't!' I begged.

'Maybe you should ring the stables,' said Katy. 'You could tell them what we're trying to do. Then maybe they wouldn't mind keeping her a bit longer.'

I desperately didn't want to ring the stables. I was terrified in case it was Mrs Foster who answered. But one of us had to ring, and I thought probably it had to be me as it was my mum who'd gone and messed up.

'Okay,' I said. 'I'll do it.'

It wasn't Mrs Foster, that was one relief. It was a girl I didn't know. One of the ones who helped out.

'Rosie?' she said. 'She's not here any more… she's gone.'

CHAPTER
4

'*Gone?*' My voice came out in a terrified squawk. 'You mean—'

'She's gone to a school over at Farley Down.'

'Oh!'

Relief flooded over me. Just for a moment I'd felt all cold and shaky and broken out into a sweat. On jellified legs I wobbled back into the sitting room, where Mum was still beavering away at her translation.

'It's all right,' I said. 'You won't have to ring the sanctuary.'

'Oh, Hannah!' Mum stopped typing and stared at me in anguish. 'They haven't—'

'No! She's gone to another stables.'

'Thank goodness for that! You'd never have forgiven me.'

'Well, I probably would,' I said, 'because I know you can't help forgetting things. I know your memory isn't what it was.' She is always telling me this. 'But I'm glad I haven't got to!'

'So am I,' said Mum. 'I would have felt so bad! I may not be as obsessed as you and Katy, but I still hate the thought of an animal being wilfully destroyed. That's a very satisfactory conclusion! Now perhaps you can sit down and concentrate on your homework.'

And she says me and Katy are obsessed! At least we admit that animals are our passion. Mum doesn't seem to realise how much she goes on (and on!) about school and homework and how important it is to study.

'I must just tell Katy,' I said.

'Well, don't be on that phone for hours!'

'I won't,' I said. 'I'm only going to *tell* her.'

I could have texted, I suppose, but it's nicer to actually talk when you have good news. I couldn't resist being just a little bit naughty, though.

When Katy answered the phone I said in these very low and tragic tones, 'Rosie has gone.' I probably shouldn't have, because suppose Katy had had a heart attack or fallen down in a faint and cracked her skull? I never thought of that at the time. I just thought how overjoyed she was going to be! It was only afterwards I felt bad about it.

'G-gone?' she quavered, just as I had when the girl at the stables had told me.

'To another school! Over at Farley Down.'

I announced it triumphantly. Farley Down was only a short bike ride away. We could easily go there and visit!

I waited for Katy to give a great screech of triumph. We had done it! We had saved Rosie! Instead, in a doom-laden voice she said, 'A *riding* school? But she's not supposed to work!'

'Oh.' I'd been so overjoyed to think that Rosie wasn't being sent to the knacker's yard that this hadn't occurred to me.

'Maybe they won't expect her to work?' I said hopefully.

'So what would they want her for?'

'Just to... go out on beginner rides?' I said.

'She was already doing that! Everybody said she wasn't earning her keep.'

'Well! I don't know,' I said. 'All I know is she's not being turned into horsemeat!'

Angrily I switched the phone off. I'd been so relieved! I'd been so sure it was good news. Now Katy had gone and spoilt everything! Why couldn't she have let me go on being happy for just a little bit longer?

I stumped grumpily off to have some tea and do my boring homework. It was maths, and I am useless at maths. So is Mum unfortunately. She can help me with almost everything else, but she says that as far as she is concerned maths is just gobbledygook. That is a Mum word: *gobbledygook*. To me maths is double gobbledygook. As a rule if I am stuck I go wailing next door to Katy, who is some kind of mathematical genius, but when you've just crossly cut someone off on the phone you can't very well ask them if they'll kindly do your maths homework for you.

I scrawled down lots of gobbledygook answers and spent the rest of the evening curled up on the sofa glumly watching television. I didn't particularly want to watch television and afterwards wished I hadn't because they had this truly horrible documentary about people killing elephants and sawing off their tusks, and all these pictures of dead elephants came flashing on to the screen before I realised what was happening. It really upset me. I went to bed feeling in total despair with the world and humankind. I also had lots of little flickers of anxiety darting to and fro about my brain. Why *had* that riding school taken Rosie? What did they want her for? What were they going to do with her?

It was another night I spent tossing and turning. I felt like battering on my bedroom wall and waking Katy. (Her bed is just the other side.) If I couldn't sleep, I didn't see why she should. I'd been happy until she'd started putting ideas into my head!

Of course I apologised the next morning; we are never mad at each other for long. Katy apologised too. She said, 'I know you thought you were giving me good news and maybe it *is* good news. Maybe she's gone to a place where they don't mind if she doesn't earn her keep.'

'Because maybe they're rich?'

'Well, either that,' said Katy, 'or they could just be like us and love animals.'

That cheered us both up. We had visions of Rosie living in a beautiful green meadow with lots of juicy grass and interesting plants for her to nibble at and trees to keep the sun off her, and a big cosy barn where she could go if it was cold. And there would be all the other horses, all the riding-school horses, to keep her company, and she would never, ever have to work again, except maybe just the odd amble through the countryside when the weather was nice.

That is how horses *ought* to live. Not shut away in stalls.

I was so happy thinking of Rosie in her field! It didn't

bother me in the least when Ms Timbrell told us to mark one another's maths homework and I got three out of ten. Katy, who was the one marking me, was far more upset than I was.

'I'm sorry,' she whispered. 'It's just all wrong!'

'Who cares?' I said. I had more important things to worry about than maths homework, and anyway no one can be good at everything.

Ms Timbrell could hardly believe it. 'Hannah Rosenthal,' she said, 'what is the matter with you?'

Earnestly I said, 'I don't think I have a mathematical type of brain.'

'Oh, don't you?' said Ms Timbrell. 'Shall I tell you what I think?'

She seemed to be waiting for an answer, so I nodded my head.

'*I* think,' said Ms Timbrell, 'that you simply don't pay attention.'

I assured her that I did, though it is true my mind does sometimes tend to drift off and that I did once find that I had filled two whole pages of my maths book with pictures of horses instead of triangles and stuff. I still don't know how it happened! I seem to go into these sort of trances.

'It is just really difficult,' I said, 'when you don't understand anything.'

'You understand that two and two make four,' said Ms Timbrell. 'At least, I take it you do?'

The Mouth sniggered.

'Yes?' said Ms Timbrell. 'Two and two make four?'

I nodded.

'In that case...' She waved my maths homework triumphantly in my face. 'How do you come to the answer *minus six* for question number two?'

Everybody in the class just fell about. Even Katy giggled. An answer of minus six was apparently ridiculous. How was I to know? I thought very hard of Rosie in her field.

'It's all gobbledygook,' I said.

'You can say that again!' said Ms Timbrell. 'Honestly, Hannah, there are times when I really do despair.'

There were times when I despaired, too, but about more important things than only getting three out of ten for my maths homework. So long as Rosie was safe I wouldn't have cared if I'd got no marks at all.

Katy told me at breaktime that she would have helped me if I'd gone round to her place, but I assured her that it was absolutely not important.

'In my list of priorities,' I said – Mum is always going on about her list of priorities, 'maths is somewhere right down at the very bottom.'

'So what's at number one?' said Katy.

I told her to take a wild guess.

'Rosie?' She nodded. 'I've been lying awake every night worrying about her!'

I said, 'Me too. Maybe now we'll be able to sleep.'

I did wake up just once in the night thinking about what Katy had said earlier – why *would* another riding school want a horse that couldn't earn its keep? – but I quickly squeezed my brain tight shut and started going through the alphabet naming animals, a is for antelope, b is for bear and so on, which is this thing I do when I want to keep the horrid thoughts at bay (like after seeing the film about the elephants being killed, or reading something upsetting in the paper).

Next morning, as we turned in through the school gates, Motormouth came clomping up to us. (Clomping is how she walks: clomp, clump, all self-important.)

'Did you hear about your horse?' she said.

Katy, immediately agitated, said, 'What?' at the same time as I said, 'Yes! She's gone to another stables.'

'Farley Down.' The Mouth looked at us pityingly. 'I wouldn't want a horse of mine going there!'

It was Katy, in a small tight voice, who said, 'Why not?'

'I just wouldn't. They've got a foul reputation!'

'Why?' I said. 'What do they do?'

'Everybody knows what they do… they run their horses into the ground.'

'But Rosie can't be used!' I said. 'Only for beginner rides.'

'They wouldn't care. They send their horses out *lame*.

And they don't feed them properly. I knew a girl that used to ride there. She had to stop because she said all their horses were knackered. It'd have been better if your one had been sent for slaughter. At least by now it would all be over.'

Well! That put paid to our happiness. We were plunged once again into deepest despair. Katy, very nobly, didn't remind me that she had had her doubts. She did her best to look on the bright side.

'You know what Motormouth's like. She just says things to get us going.'

'That's what we thought before,' I wailed. 'When she said about Rosie being sent to the knacker's!'

'Well, and she was wrong, wasn't she? Because it hasn't happened!'

'No, she's just been sent to some horrible place that's going to work her to death!'

'We don't actually know that,' said Katy. 'She could just be making it up.'

But I had a horrible feeling she wasn't. When someone

has their own pony and moves in horsey circles they get to hear about these things.

'Mrs Foster wouldn't have let them take her if they weren't going to treat her properly,' said Katy.

'She might if they gave her some money,' I said. 'Or even if they just came and took her for free. She was going to have to *pay* the knacker people.'

'Really?' Katy looked frightened. She obviously hadn't known that. It was something that Bethany had told me.

'Let's go to the stables after school,' I said, 'and see what we can find out.'

We had to go home first, as always, to stop our mums having panic attacks.

'We're just going to the stables,' I told Mum.

Of course she wanted to know why, so I just babbled some gobbledygook story about how we wanted to do a bit of research and went rushing off before she could start digging too deeply. I knew if I told her the real reason she'd only roll her eyes and go, 'Oh, Hannah, for goodness' sake! I thought that was all sorted?' Maybe it was. Maybe the Mouth *had* just been making things up. Oh, I did hope so!

We found Bethany at the stables. She said, 'Hi, you two! Good news about Rosie. Did you hear?'

Katy and me looked at each other and grinned. Bethany thought it was good news! So much for Motormouth.

All the same, now that we were there I thought we should make certain.

'They won't work her to death,' I said, 'will they?'

'They shouldn't be working her at all! They know she's got damaged lungs.'

'Just beginner rides,' I said.

'Yes, and maybe a bit of ring work.'

'Are they rich?' said Katy.

Bethany looked bewildered. 'Rich?'

'Or just animal lovers,' I said.

'Oh! I see what you mean. I don't know. I don't know much about them. What makes you ask?'

'Someone told us they rode their horses into the ground,' I mumbled.

Bethany frowned. 'Maybe they used to. I believe they've recently changed hands. I'm sure Pippa wouldn't have let her go there if she didn't think she was going to be looked after.'

There was a silence. I did *so* want to be convinced!

'Who told you, anyway?' said Bethany.

I said, 'The M— I mean, Tara.'

'Oh! Well! Tara. She's a bit of a doom merchant. I shouldn't worry about it, if I were you. At least it's not the knacker's yard!'

She smiled hopefully, but Katy didn't say anything and neither did I.

'Okay, well! See you at the weekend? Same time as usual?'

Katy opened her mouth to say yes, but I stepped in very smartly. 'We can't make it this weekend.'

Katy looked at me in surprise. 'Why can't we?' she hissed, as we left the stables.

'Because I had a sudden thought... I think we ought to go and ride at Farley Down.'

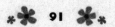

'Farley Down? Why?'

Katy may be a mathematical genius but there are times when she is *really* slow on the uptake.

'So we can check on Rosie,' I said. 'Make sure she's all right.'

'Oh! Of course.' Katy brightened. 'Good idea!'

'I'll ring up and book,' I said.

'Tell them I want something gentle,' pleaded Katy. 'I don't want to be put on a racehorse!'

She needn't have worried: there weren't any racehorses at Farley Down. It was a mean, miserable sort of place. The Mouth hadn't been making up stories; I hated it the minute I saw it! The yard was covered in hay and horse dung and bits of machinery. And all the poor horses were kept in stalls so narrow they could hardly turn round. They couldn't have turned round anyway, because they were tethered with their heads facing the far end so they had nothing to stare at but a bare blank wall. It is *cruel* to keep horses tied up like that.

One of the first things we saw was a handwritten notice that said **TIOLET. TURN OF THE ******
LIGHT! (signed) G. Chislett, Prop.** (I put the row of stars as they spelt out a word that I am not allowed to use, but which I wouldn't anyway as Mum says people only swear when they run out of vocabulary. I never run out of vocabulary!)

Katy, in mystified tones, asked me what a prop was. I had to admit I wasn't quite sure but thought it probably meant he was the owner.

'Whatever he is,' I said, 'he obviously can't spell.' *And* he obviously didn't have a very good vocabulary. Imagine pinning up such a rude sort of notice!

'Do you think that's him?' whispered Katy.

A small, scrawny man had just come out of a dilapidated shed, which was obviously the office. He was shouting angrily at someone across the yard.

'I thought I ****** told you to get that ****** horse tacked up?'

'I'm sorry, Mr Chislett!' A girl came backing out of

one of the boxes. Her face was bright red; she looked almost on the verge of tears. 'I couldn't get him to stand still!'

'Couldn't get him to ****** stand still? What do I ****** pay you for?'

I honestly thought, for a moment, that he was going to burst at the seams, his rage was so immense. Katy and I exchanged horrified glances. This horrible violent man was now in charge of our beloved Rosie?

I'd been anxiously looking all around but I couldn't see Rosie anywhere, though lots of the stalls were empty so maybe, I thought, she had been allowed into the field. Not that it was much of a field, but better than being shut away in a dingy stall.

Two tatty-looking ponies were brought out for me and Katy. They were called Dusty and Solo and they were such a pathetic pair. I felt so sorry for them! They made Jet and Freya seem like quality (which we knew they weren't because the Mouth had taken care to tell us).

The girl who took us out was called Natalie. She was

old Chislett's daughter. She didn't look much like her dad as she was quite long and skinny, but she obviously had his sweet nature, ha ha. (That is a joke.) She was really sullen and hardly talked at all. And the ride was dead boring! Those poor ponies didn't even want to trot, let alone canter. And I think they'd totally forgotten what it felt like to enjoy a good gallop. Katy was probably quite relieved, but I began to understand how the Mouth had felt that first day when Bethany wouldn't let her take off.

I pushed and prodded until Dusty broke into a reluctant half trot and I was able to catch up with Natalie.

'Have you got a horse called Rosie?' I said.

'Dunno,' said Natalie. 'I've been away for a few days. What's she like?'

'She's a strawberry roan,' I said. Despite being so worried, I couldn't help feeling just a little bit proud of my new horsey knowledge. 'About sixteen hands?'

'Oh, yeah! I remember. She's out on a hack.'

Cold hands clawed at my heart.

'Out on a *hack*?'

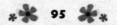

'Yeah. Why?'

'She's not supposed to be used like that! She's got damaged lungs.'

'Yeah?'

'She was in a fire! She's only fit for beginner rides.'

'Who says?'

'It's true! Honestly!'

Natalie turned and looked me up and down. 'What are you? Some kind of expert?'

I felt like telling her I was an official Animal Samaritan, but I guessed she would only sneer.

'My dad's been around horses all his life,' she said. 'He knows what he's doing.'

I swallowed. 'Why does he keep them all tied up?'

'Makes it easier to muck out.'

'But don't they get bored? They've got nothing to look at! And they can't talk to each other.'

'They get enough to do,' said Natalie.

She was one of those people it is impossible to have a proper conversation with. I grew more and more worried about poor Rosie. I fell back and waited for Katy, who couldn't make Solo move any faster than a slow walk.

'This is horrible,' said Katy. 'I feel mean just sitting on him!'

I felt exactly the same. You can always tell when a horse is well fed and well looked after; they are always eager to go. When I rode Jet, it was almost impossible to hold him back. Give him his head and he would have gone the whole ride at a gallop! Dusty had been reluctant even to break into a trot.

With a heavy heart I said it looked as if the Mouth had been right. 'These stables are *vile!*'

'Did you ask about Rosie?'

I said, 'Yes. She's out on a hack.'

'On a *hack?*'

I nodded, and my hat almost fell off. All the hats at Farley Down seemed to be either too big or too small. Bethany wouldn't have let us go out wearing hats that didn't fit, but at Farley Down they obviously didn't care.

Didn't care about the hats, didn't care about the horses. They were rubbish! Worse than rubbish. They were that thing that politicians are always on about: *not fit for purpose.* If there was any justice in the world, they would be closed down. But there isn't, of course; there isn't any justice. Not for animals. They are skinned for their fur and shot for their tusks and poisoned in laboratories and sometimes it all gets too much and I *just can't bear it.*

'What are we going to do?' whispered Katy.

I wiped my nose on the back of my hand and said that I didn't know, except that we had to do *something.* We were Animal Samaritans; we couldn't just sit back and pretend nothing was happening.

The nightmare ride came to an end at last. We clopped back into the filthy stable yard and Natalie took the ponies and led them away, back to captivity in their tiny cramped stalls. We were about to go to the office and pay when there was a clattering of hooves and we saw the hack returning. They were cantering, flat out, down the lane. Amongst them was Rosie.

Our poor sweet darling Rosie! A huge great red-faced man was sitting on her. He looked like a heavyweight wrestler. All the other horses snorted and tossed their heads as they pulled up in the yard, but not Rosie. I have never seen a poor horse look so dejected. She stood there, drooping, the picture of horsey misery. Her head was down, her flanks were heaving. She was covered in sweat.

Before I even had time to stop and think about it, I had gone rushing forward.

'That horse has damaged lungs!' I shouted. 'She shouldn't be ridden like that!'

CHAPTER 5

A silence fell over the yard. Everyone was looking at me. The huge great brute of a man slowly dismounted, and, oh, I was so relieved. At least it meant poor Rosie could breathe a bit easier.

I stroked her neck, all flecked with white foam, while the other riders just sat there gaping. That sweet girl was trembling, her ears pulled right back. A sure sign of horsey distress.

The big brutish man said, 'We'll see about this,' and went stamping off across the yard.

'Oh, Rosie!' I whispered. I kissed her soft velvety nose and she did her best to nuzzle me. Then I put my finger in her mouth and wobbled her lower lip for her, the way she liked, but she didn't push her head against me or flicker her ears as she used to. She was too tired, and too unhappy.

Natalie had appeared. She yanked Rosie's bridle away from me. Then she gave me this absolutely filthy look and said, 'You'd do better to mind your own business.'

'But look at her!' I cried. 'She shouldn't be ridden like that!'

'What's it to you?' said Natalie. 'What do you know about anything?'

I opened my mouth to say that I was an Animal Samaritan and had sworn an oath to fight for animals, but before I could get any further than 'I'm an An—' there was the sound of shouting and old Chisel came roaring into the yard. He had a rake in his hand and he was making straight for me.

'What the devil is going on?' he bawled. 'Who the hell do you think you are, poxy well coming here, laying down the law?'

Katy said later that she was sorry she waited so long to say anything. 'But you were doing so well! And I did come and stand next to you.' She added that 'The man is obviously a complete lunatic,' and that she thought I had been really brave.

I have to say that I didn't feel very brave. It was actually rather scary the way old Chislett was waving that rake around. His eyes had gone all bulgy, as if they were about to come bursting out of their sockets, and I could see a vein in his neck leaping about like a big worm under his skin. I suppose if I am honest I would have to admit that what I really felt like doing was jumping on my bike and cycling away just as fast as I could. It was only the sight of poor exhausted Rosie, standing there with her head hanging down, that gave me courage.

'Look at her!' I pleaded. 'She's not well!'

All the other people had got off their horses and were looking the other way, obviously not wanting to be a part of it. Old Chisel turned and glared, as if daring them to say anything. Then he turned and jabbed the rake at Natalie.

'Get that poxy horse back in its box! And you –' he prodded at me – 'get out of my yard! If you ever come here again, spreading lies about my horses, I'll have your guts for garters! I'll have you up for slander!'

The big red-faced man was hovering, trying to get a word in. 'Jeff, Jeff!'

'What's your problem?' snarled Chisel.

'It's not true, is it? About the horse?'

'Of course it's not poxy well true! What do you think? I send my customers out on poxy knackered horses? You take her poxy word before mine?'

'No. No!' Red Face backed away. 'I just wanted to make sure.'

'Well! Now you have.'

'Yes.' Red Face flapped a hand. 'I'll – ah – see you next week.'

Red Face disappeared. All the other riders had disappeared. Me and Katy were the only ones left.

'She really has got damaged lungs,' I whispered.

'So? What do you want me to do about it? Send her for horsemeat?'

'Just treat her *gently*,' I begged.

'Listen, you poxy little pipsqueak!' He pointed at me with the rake. 'These are animals. They are here to be ridden. And as long as they are capable of being ridden, they will be ridden. End of story. Right? You got that? Do I make myself clear? Now, hoppit!'

'*Please*,' I said.

He swung round. 'Are you thick or something? Didn't you just hear what I said?'

Katy clutched at my arm. I shook her off. 'We're Animal Samaritans!' I cried. 'We've sworn to protect animals! We can't just walk away and do nothing!'

'No?' He stuck his face close to mine. 'So what are you planning?'

I could have said we were going to report him to the RSPCA, but somehow I didn't think it would bother him too much. He looked like the sort of man who was always being reported and always got away with it.

'If we found a s-sanctuary,' I stammered, 'would you let her g-go?'

'Well, now! That would all depend.'

'On wh-what?' I said. I didn't like the expression that had come slithering into his eyes. All mean and grasping. It made him seem even nastier than when he was shouting four-letter words.

'On how much you'd be prepared to give me.'

'*G-give* you?' I said.

'Well, you didn't think I'd let her go for nothing, did you? I paid good money for that horse!'

'How much?' said Katy, suddenly springing into action.

'Well… let's see. He rubbed a hand over his sandpapery chin. 'I reckon she's still got a few weeks' work left in her. So it's not just a question of how much I paid, but how much I could make.'

'*How much?*' That was Katy again. She had really come to life!

'Say… three hundred?'

I gulped. 'P-pounds?' Three hundred *pounds?*'

Our dismay must have shown in our faces.

'Take it or leave it. But don't set foot in my stable again spreading vicious lies amongst my customers or you'll be in trouble. *Dead* trouble. I mean it!'

Katy and I went out, reeling. I felt like I had just been punched in the stomach.

'Three hundred pounds!'

We could never hope to find so much money. I had never even *seen* so much money!

'We could get a bit of it,' said Katy.

'A bit's not enough,' I wailed. 'He said *three hundred.*'

'Maybe we could pay by instalments.'

'Oh!' I hadn't thought of that. Katy is just so brilliant when it comes to money matters. She even understands stuff such as rates of interest and returns on investment, which to me is just like – well! Gobbledygook. 'D'you think he'd let us?'

'Only one way to find out,' said Katy.

'You mean—'

'Go back and ask him.'

'What, m-me?' I said.

'Well... one of us.'

There was a pause.

'I'll do it,' said Katy. She pushed her bike at me. 'Hold that!'

'Be careful,' I begged. 'He might hurt you!'

By way of reply Katy just tossed her head and made a gesture that some of the boys in our class make when they want to shock you. Not that they shock me! I am unshockable. But I was quite surprised at Katy. Being an Animal Samaritan had made her quite ferocious. When we first became friends she was ever so timid. I was the one that always went rushing in. Katy was the one that did all the thinking and came up with all the good arguments. These days she goes rushing in just as bold as can be.

I stood there holding our bikes and wondering what I would do if I heard the sound of screaming. Should I go to her rescue or jump on my bike and madly pedal off to get help? Our mums would be furious! They tell us over and over 'not to interfere in things that are no concern of yours'. But animals were our concern! Rosie in particular.

I jiggled about from one foot to the other, wishing that Katy would come back.

From where I was I could see across the horrible littered yard to the box where Rosie had been taken. I could see Natalie in there with her. She seemed to be rubbing her down, and I was relieved about that. I could remember Bethany telling us that it was bad to let a horse stay covered in sweat. But I still hated the thought of having to go away and leave that poor suffering horse in the hands of such loathsome people. She must be so confused and frightened!

Katy still hadn't come back. I was just beginning to think that I would have to pluck up the courage to go after her, when, thank goodness, she reappeared. She didn't *look* as if she had been attacked. At any rate she wasn't covered in blood.

'Are you all right?' I whispered.

'Yes!' She grabbed her bike and threw herself on to it. 'He said if we managed to find the first two hundred, he'd let us have her and we could pay off the rest on hire purchase… a bit every week.'

'Oh! That's wonderful,' I said.

'He wanted to charge us ten per cent interest but I beat him down to five, which is *bad enough* but at least it's better than ten.'

'No, no, it's brilliant!' I said. I stared at her admiringly. 'I would never have thought of that!''

Now all we had to do was find a couple of hundred pounds… *urgently*. We couldn't bear the thought of our poor frightened girl having to stay in that horsey hell a minute longer than necessary.

We discussed all the ways we could think of for making money.

Katy said that she would ask her dad. 'He might give us some. And my mum, perhaps.' She sounded a bit more doubtful about her mum. Mrs Cooper is not at *all* an animal person. Not that she would ever be cruel to them; she just doesn't think they're as important as human beings.

I said sadly that there wasn't much point in me asking my mum as I knew she didn't have any.

'I have some money in some bond things,' said Katy. 'But they won't let me get at it until I'm twenty-one.'

'I don't have anything at all,' I said. I didn't even know what bond things *were*.

'Maybe…' Katy wrinkled her brow. 'Maybe we could use our riding money? Like, save it each week instead of going riding?'

'Without telling our mums?'

'Well…' Katy pulled a face. She obviously didn't feel comfortable about it. I didn't, either; I hated the thought of deceiving Mum. She had been so happy when she'd told me that at long last I could have my riding lessons! Riding lessons for me, new football kit for Benjy. Almost nothing for herself. She hadn't even had her hair done, which was something she'd been talking about for simply ages.

'Oh, what does it matter?' she'd said. 'It's only vanity!'

But I reckoned that Mum deserved to be a bit vain once in a while.

'I really *hate* the idea of giving money to that loathsome man,' I said.

'So do I,' said Katy.

We both sighed. There are times when you just have to grit your teeth. Even if it *did* mean deceiving our mums. After all, it was to save a horse's life. A poor, innocent, ill-used horse who had never hurt anyone but just done her best to please.

I reminded Katy of this and she said that I was quite right; we were Animal Samaritans and the animals must come first. We had to think of Rosie, not worry about where we were getting the money from.

'Just so long as we get it. That's all that matters.'

There was a bit of a silence before I said, 'So where is it going to come from?'

'Well, if we use next week's riding money, that's forty pounds before we even start! Then there's our pocket money, five for you, six for me, that's another eleven pounds, which makes fifty-one. Then if our mums would let us have a week's pocket money *in advance*, that would make sixty-two… that would only leave…' I could see her doing quick calculations in her head. 'That would only leave a hundred and thirty-eight!'

'*Only?*' I said.

'Well, it's a start,' said Katy. 'And that's without even trying!'

'So where do we get the rest?' My voice came out in a plaintive wail. Katy rolled her eyes. 'I'm sorry,' I said, 'it's just that I've never even *had* a hundred and thirty-eight pounds!'

'Me neither,' said Katy. 'Except in these silly bond things that I'm not allowed to touch. But it can't be that difficult!'

We pedalled furiously up the lane.

'Maybe,' I said, 'we could sell things?'

'*Yesss!*' Katy, triumphant, raised a clenched fist. 'That's a brilliant idea!'

'Let's go home and find something!'

We cycled home as fast as our pedals would take us.

'Meet you in half an hour,' I said.

The minute I got in I was ambushed by Benjy wanting to show me another drawing that he'd done. I gave it a brief glance and said, 'Yes, lovely! What is it?'

Benjy said it was 'an aminal'.

I didn't wait to find out what kind of an aminal. I didn't even correct him to 'animal'. I said, 'Sorry, I'm in a bit of a rush,' and set off up the stairs. Almost immediately Mum's voice called after me: '*HannAH!*'

Bother. Now what?

'Mum, I've got things to do!' I yelled.

'Could you just stop for a moment, please?'

I ground my teeth. Sometimes a person just cannot call their life their own.

'What is it?'

'Don't you take that tone of voice with me!' said Mum. 'I thought we'd made a bargain? In return for your pocket money… *what was it you were going to do?*'

'Make-sure-I-dusted-and-vacuumed-my-room-and-put-my-things-away, which I promise I'm going to do just as soon as I've done something else, which is really, really urgent! Oh, and, Mum…' I turned at the top of the stairs, putting on my sweetest smile. 'Do you think you could let me have two weeks' pocket money in advance?'

'No,' said Mum. 'I don't think you deserve it. What do you want it for, anyway?'

'Well… I, um… I need it,' I said. I didn't want to tell her that it was part of the ransom money we had to pay to that hideous horrible man. She would only get in a fuss and start worrying in case we got into trouble.

'What do you need it *for*?' said Mum.

'Just things.'

'What things?'

I groaned inside my head. 'I just want to buy something,' I said. 'A horsey thing.' Well, it was sort of true. I mean, if a horse isn't a horsey thing, what is? 'It's going cheap,' I said. 'It's only on offer for a short while.'

And that probably *was* true. I just couldn't see our

poor darling Rosie lasting much longer the way she was being treated.

'Mum, *please*,' I said. 'It's *desperate*!'

'I'll think about it,' said Mum. 'When you've cleaned up all the mess in your room.'

I flew upstairs with Benjy hot on my heels, wanting me to look again at his drawing and guess what animal it was. I told him that I was sorry, I really didn't have the time.

'I'll look later, I promise! Right now there's something *very serious* that I have to do. Katy and I are trying to make some money to rescue a poor sick horse. We're looking for things that we can sell. It's really urgent! But whatever you do, you mustn't tell Mum. It's a secret. Okay? Just you and me!'

Benjy solemnly promised that he wouldn't breathe a word. He said that he had some things I could sell.

'Shall I go and get them?'

I said yes, all right, and he went scampering happily off, leaving me to see what I could uncover amongst all the mess and the muddle that somehow seemed to have accumulated in my bedroom. *I* don't know where it all comes from! It just gathers. And most of it, sadly, the sort of rubbishy stuff that no one would want to buy. But I had to have *something*! I knew it wasn't any use taking clothes, even ones I did my best never to wear. Mum would be bound to notice they'd gone. It would be, 'Whatever happened to that little cardigan Nan knitted?' or 'Where is that dress we got you for Auntie Susan's wedding?' Yuck, yuck, yuck!

In the end all I could come up with were a few books (ones I'd grown out of), some china ornaments that I was really reluctant to part with (I had to keep reminding myself that Rosie was far more important), a bar of soap in the shape of a cow that I'd never been able to bring myself to use, and a few odd bits and pieces, such as jigsaw puzzles and painting sets and stuff, that had been at the back of my cupboard for so long I reckoned Mum was sure to have forgotten about them.

I had just fetched a big carrier bag from the kitchen

and packed everything into it (quickly, quickly before Mum could appear and ask me what I was doing) when Benjy staggered in carrying his entire wardrobe: T-shirts, sweatshirts, shorts, jeans. Even shoes and socks! He dumped it all on my bed and proudly announced that it was for 'the poor sick horse'. I didn't know what to say! I didn't want to hurt his feelings but I had to explain that Mum would go demented if I sold all his clothes.

We took them back to his room and he let me help myself to a few books and toys instead. He was so anxious to help the poor sick horse! I really think that one day, when he is old enough, he will become an Animal Samaritan himself.

Katy was waiting for me with a big holdall. She had had the same problem as I had, trying to find stuff that her mum wouldn't miss. We agreed that our mums probably had loads of stuff of their own that they didn't really need any more but neither of us had liked to ask for fear of them finding out about old Chislett and how he was holding our poor Rosie to ransom.

'Mum told me just the other day,' said Katy, 'that I was taking this whole animal thing too far.'

'Yes, mine says that,' I agreed.

'But how *can* you take it too far?' said Katy. 'Most people don't take it far enough!'

'Most people,' I said bitterly, 'don't take it anywhere at all.'

We staggered up the road with our bags and headed for the indoor market that is held every weekend. What we thought we'd do, we'd go go round all the stalls and ask the stall owners if they were interested. We would see who offered the best price.

'I mean, *look*,' said Katy, opening her bag to show me. 'A padded coat hanger!'

I said, 'What's a padded coat hanger?'

'It's a coat hanger that's padded... It's even got a little bag of smelly stuff hanging off it.'

'Cool!'

'Well, people do seem to like them,' said Katy. 'Mum's got so many I didn't think she'd miss just one. Oh, and, look, a bottle of perfume! Mum just opened it to have a sniff. It's called Bijou of the Orient. I should think anyone would want that!'

'And my china ornaments,' I said.

Well! You would have thought so. I don't know what is wrong with people. Those were *good* ornaments. There was a little squirrel eating a nut and a little donkey pulling a cart and the cutest little bunny wearing a red suit. Okay, so maybe the donkey had a chip out of one of his ears, but it hardly showed. Yet all we got, for the books, and the ornaments, and the padded coat hanger, not to mention all the other lovely things we'd lugged with us, was a measly five pounds! I would have thought we'd get *at least* twenty.

Katy was a bit despondent about it as well, though she bravely tried to look on the bright side.

'At least it's five pounds more than we did have.'

'But we'll never get enough at this rate!' I wailed. 'I haven't got anything else I can sell!'

'No.' Katy stamped viciously on an empty Coke can

and squashed it flat. 'There've got to be other ways of making money!'

We agreed that we would meet up next day and discuss it. Then we would write out a list: **WAYS OF MAKING MONEY.**

'And then,' said Katy, 'we'll try them all, one after another, until we get enough!'

CHAPTER 6

In the end I had to tell Mum why it was I wanted my pocket money in advance. She said that a vague 'horsey thing' wasn't good enough.

'Be more specific!'

I said, '*Why?* Why do I have to?' I could hear my voice, all whiny and protesting.

Mum said, 'I want to be sure you're not frittering it away on something stupid.'

I felt like shouting, 'It's my money! I can fritter it if I want!' But I knew it would only make her angry and tell me *not to take that tone of voice.*

'Well?' said Mum.

I heaved a sigh and mumbled, 'It's for Rosie.'

'Not again!' cried Mum. 'I thought that was all settled?'

I said, 'Well, it's not! They're not looking after her properly. Mum, they're *killing* her! They just don't care! And she's all tied up in a horrid little box where she can't even turn round. It's like a prison cell!'

'Maybe horses don't mind being tied up,' said Mum.

'They do! They hate it! It's not right! They ought to be free to run about. You shouldn't *ever* keep a horse tied up so it can't move! It's wicked! It's—'

'All right, all right!' Mum threw up her hands. 'I give in! You don't have to lecture me. Just tell me what you're planning to do with this money you're asking for.'

I brightened. 'We're going to buy her back!'

'With two weeks' pocket money?'

'Well... no. We'll need a bit more than that.'

'A good bit more, I should think!'

'We're going to discuss it this morning.'

'*After* you've done your homework.'

'Oh, well, yes! Of course,' I said, doing my best to

sound all keen and eager. 'Of course we'll do our homework *first*.'

'Hm!' said Mum.

'I don't suppose *you* have any ideas how to make money?' I said.

Mum gave what I think is called a mirthless laugh.

'Please,' I begged. 'This is serious!'

Mum said, 'Oh, Hannah, making money is always serious. I spend my entire life struggling to make money! I'm sorry, sweetheart, I really don't know what to suggest.'

Glumly I reported this to Katy. She said, 'Hey, guess what? I just had an idea!'

I looked at her hopefully.

'Maybe we could do that crowdfunding thing… you know? When you go on the internet and ask people to send you money? You can raise thousands that way!'

I hesitated.

Katy said, '*Well?*'

I said, 'Mm… I s'pose.' I didn't mean to throw cold water on her suggestion but I felt instinctively doubtful. It just sounded too easy!

Katy was obviously a bit annoyed. She said, 'What d'you mean, you *suppose*? It's what people do! They do it all the time! Look.' She typed something into Google. 'See? GoFundMe… all you have to do…'

All you had to do was set up an account. We tried! We typed in the name of Mum's bank, and the name of Katy's mum's bank, we even put in details of Katy's bond thing that she wasn't allowed to touch, but none of it was any good. I wailed that I'd known it was too easy!

'That's no reason to give in.' Katy said it very fiercely. 'We just need a grown-up, that's all. Someone with a bank account… ask your mum! See if she'll set it up for us.'

'Why not ask yours?' I said.

'Well, I could try,' said Katy, 'but you know what she's like… She doesn't care about animals. She just doesn't think they're important. Yours,' she assured me, 'is far more likely to be sympathetic.'

Mum usually was quite sympathetic; just not when she was struggling to finish a translation so that she could pay some bills.

'Oh, Hannah, please!' she cried. 'Not now! If I don't get this thing off double quick, we're going to be in trouble! If it's that important, why not try asking your friend at the sanctuary?'

That was what it always came back to: why didn't we ask Meg? But as Katy sadly reminded me, when I suggested it to her, Meg was away trying to raise money for her own animals.

'She's doing this walking thing.'

'A sponsored walk!' I looked at Katy, suddenly excited. 'Maybe that's what we could do?'

'What, walk?'

'Why not?'

'Where would we do it?'

'Anywhere! Round the playing field.'

'But who'd sponsor us?'

'Your mum – my mum – your dad. You were *going* to ask your dad—'

'I will!' said Katy. 'I'll ring him tonight. That still only makes three people. *They're* not going to give us enough money!'

'People at school,' I said. 'Mrs B. The lady in the newsagent's. The milkman, the postman... anybody! What we need to do, we need to print out some forms and get people to put their names down saying how much they'll sponsor us for. I can print them out on Mum's computer. No problem! Then we can ask people to fill them in and then all we have to do is just walk. Write it down! You're supposed to be making a list.'

Obediently Katy picked up her pen and wrote, **WAYS TO MAKE MONEY** on a page torn from my homework book. Then: **No. 1 Sponsered Walk.**

'Actually it's spelt with an O,' I said. 'Not that it matters.'

'Then why mention it?' snapped Katy.

Honestly, she is *so* oversensitive. She didn't have to bite my head off!

'Think of other things,' I said.

We sat and thought. Katy chewed her pen, I chewed my thumbnail. Every now and again Katy would go, 'We could always—' And I would go, 'What?' And Katy would go, 'No. That's no use!'

If it wasn't Katy, it was me.

'How about—'

'What?'

'No! That wouldn't work.'

'We've got to think of *something*!' cried Katy.

'I know!' I sprang up. A brilliant idea had come to me. 'If we cycled out to Sainsbury's, we could make a fortune offering to take people's shopping trolleys back for them.'

Katy wrinkled her brow. 'Do people want their shopping trolleys taken back?'

'Well,' I said, 'they might do. If they were old, or parked miles away, or had sprained their ankles or – or had little kids or...'

Katy was giving me that look she gets when she reckons I'm talking rubbish.

'I always take Mum's back,' I said. 'She says it's really helpful. And she's not even old!'

'So how often do you go shopping with your mum?' said Katy.

I said, 'Well… now and again. Stop being so negative! Let's just go and do it.'

'What, right away?'

'Why not? It's a good time! It's what people do on a Sunday. They go to the supermarket! And there's the DIY shop as well. We could make *oodles*.'

Katy still seemed a bit hesitant, but as she obviously couldn't think of anything better she reluctantly agreed to give it a go.

I said to Mum, 'After we've been to the stables…' I couldn't bring myself to say, 'After we've been for a ride.' It was bad enough taking my riding money off her, without telling a whopping great lie, pretending we were going for a ride when we actually weren't. 'We're going to go to Sainsbury's,' I said, 'to ask people if we can put their shopping trolleys away for them.' And, of course, give us something for our trouble. I reckoned the least people would be willing to give was 50p. Maybe even a pound if they were feeling generous. It would soon mount up!

'Well, just be polite about it,' said Mum. 'Don't make a nuisance of yourselves.'

The Sainsbury's car park was simply swarming, just as I'd known it would be. So was the DIY shop next door. But Sainsbury's, I thought, was the more promising.

Katy and I chained our bikes to some railings and set off.

'I suppose,' quavered Katy, 'that this is all right?'

I said, 'Of course it's all right! We're not going to *mug* anyone. Just ask if we can park their trolleys for them.'

'But I don't know what to say!'

'Look, I'll show you,' I said. 'Nothing to it!'

I marched up to two women that were standing talking. One of them had a full trolley; she was obviously going back to put everything into her car. The other had an empty trolley; she had obviously just *come* from her car.

'Excuse me,' I said, ever so polite. 'Would you like me to take your trolley back for you?'

'Take it back?' The woman laughed. 'I've only just got it!'

'Oh.' I felt my cheeks fire up.

'What happened?' said Katy.

'Nothing! She hadn't done any shopping yet. I'll try another one.'

This time I went up to an old lady who I could see had trouble walking.

'Excuse me,' I said. 'Have you already done your shopping?'

That old lady! She got hold of *quite* the wrong end of the stick.

She said, 'I have, my dear. It's yours if you want it.' And she beamed and pushed the trolley at me as if she was doing me a good turn.

I knew that Katy was watching, all ready to say I told you so. *Told you it wouldn't work!*

'Really, I meant could I just take it back for you,' I gabbled. 'Because it's a long way to walk and I thought maybe you'd like someone else to do it, instead of you having to.'

'Oh! Well, that's very kind,' said the old lady. 'Thank you so much!'

With that, she turned and started to walk off. Desperately I called after her: 'I'm an Animal Samaritan!' I jabbed a finger on my badge, so she could see that I was genuine. 'I'm trying to raise money to help a poor sick horse!'

That old lady turned out to be ace. She understood at once what I was saying!

'Ah,' she said, 'you're collecting. You really ought to have a proper collecting tin, but never mind. You're saving my legs, so I'm not complaining! Here you are.' She pressed a coin into my hand. 'For the poor sick horse. Every little helps!'

She'd only given me 20p but perhaps, I thought, it was all she could afford. At least it was a start!

After that, I told everyone what I was collecting for. Some people were sympathetic, but lots couldn't have cared less. A few were really horrible. They not only didn't give me anything but told me I ought to be ashamed of myself: 'Pestering people!'

Katy came up to me almost in tears because one woman had been extra specially mean.

'She said she had a good mind to call the police!'

'Well, she can call them as much as she wants,' I said, 'we're not doing anything wrong. It's a free country! All we're doing is just trying to earn a bit of money. It's not like *begging*. We're offering a service!'

Katy sniffed, and scrubbed at her eyes. 'How much longer do we have to stay?'

Poor Katy! She really hates having to go up to complete strangers and talk to them. It doesn't bother me; I'll talk to anyone. The nastier some people were, the more determined I became. I reminded Katy that it

was for Rosie. I said, 'Think of that poor frightened horse shut up in her prison cell… we've *got* to get enough money to rescue her!'

We stayed at Sainsbury's until five o'clock, by which time even I thought we had better get back home before our mums started on their panic attacks. In any case I didn't want Katy reduced to a nervous wreck! We still had our sponsored walk to do.

'How much have we made?' said Katy.

We turned out our pockets. Katy had made six pounds and an old French franc that some cheating person had given her: I had made £10.20. Katy promised that she would make out proper accounts as soon as she'd had her tea.

'We have to keep a note of everything.'

'*And* somewhere to keep all the money!'

Katy said she knew where we could put it. She said she had an old moneybox her gran had given her. 'It's got a proper lock and key!'

'So where will you keep the key?'

Katy said she would put the key on a piece of string and tie it round her neck.

'What about when we have to change for PE? They might think it's jewellery and confiscate it!'

In that case, Katy said, she would hide it in her old teddy bear. She said some of the stitches had come undone and she would simply slip the key in there.

'No problem!'

'So long as it doesn't disappear deep inside and you can't get it out again.'

'So I'll leave the string hanging out! Okay?'

She was beginning to sound a bit irritable. I didn't *want* to keep raising objections, but someone has to think of these things. She wouldn't be very happy if she had to cut open her teddy bear to get the key back.

'*Okay?*'

I didn't say, 'Suppose your mum sees it and decides to investigate?' It seemed wisest not to. So I told her that was an excellent idea and we happily parted company.

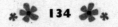

When I got in, Mum asked me how we'd done. Proudly I announced that we had made £16.20 and a French franc.

'Oh dear!' said Mum. 'That's not a very good return for all your hard work.'

I was a bit disappointed when she said that. I thought we'd done quite well! I said, 'It's sixteen pounds twenty that we didn't have before.'

'That is certainly one way of looking at it,' said Mum. 'Here!' She reached for her bag. 'Let me at least make it up to seventeen pounds for you.'

I hesitated.

'What's the matter?' said Mum. 'Not accepting charity?'

'We'll accept *anything*,' I said. 'But I wanted you to sponsor us for our sponsored walk!'

I told Mum what we were planning and she laughed and said she thought she could probably afford to sponsor us *and* make up our hard-earned money to £17. She was in a really good mood! (This was because she had finished her rush-job translation.) She even helped me work out the words to put on our sponsor form.

KATY AND HANNAH are going on a SPONSORED WALK to raise money for a POOR SICK HORSE. Please help!

And then there were three columns:

Name –   Signature   –   Amount per lap (round the sports field)

Mum filled in her name and wrote '50p' in the last column, and I then took the form next door for Katy's mum, who asked us how many laps we thought we'd do.

'Oh, loads!' said Katy.

Katy had become quite cheerful since having her tea and making up the accounts. Her mum used to be a bookkeeping person, so Katy knows about that sort of thing. She'd written it all out in her tiny neat handwriting (mine is rather large and sprawling).

FUND TO RESCUE ROSIE

Amount needed £200.00

Amount collected:

Riding money £40.00

Pocket money £11.00

Sale of Goods £5.00

Money from car park £16.20

Total £72.20

Amount still needed £127.80

'And Mum just gave me eighty p,' I said, so Katy promptly added that to the list as well.

'We're getting there!' She announced it triumphantly. 'Seventy-three pounds and we've only just started! But remember,' she hissed, 'these accounts are confidential!'

The reason they were confidential was that we were deceiving our mums. *They* didn't know what we were planning to do with our riding money. I still felt bad about it, especially with Mum having given me that 80p, but this was a question of life and death. Plus I had sworn a solemn oath that I would always do my best to help an animal in need. Mum surely wouldn't want me to break my word?

On Monday morning we took our sponsor forms into school and went round everyone in our class asking if they would sponsor us. Every single person did! Even a creep like Kevin Bone, who does nothing but make trouble, was shamed into it. He only put himself down for 1p per lap, and sniggered as if he thought he was being funny, but we were not too proud to accept it. Even that obnoxious pair Motormouth and her friend Caley finally gave in and added their names. They weren't going to, not to begin with. When we first approached them they just sneered and started off on their 'Why do you only care about animals?' routine. But then Katy, very bold, went up to Mr O'Sullivan and asked him if *he* would sponsor us, and he said he would be only too happy to do so and put his name down for a whole pound. A pound for every lap we completed! Most people had only put 10p or even just 5p. Needless to say, once they discovered that Mr O'Sullivan was supporting us the obnoxious pair couldn't wait to add their names.

'We have decided,' said Caley.

'We have come to a decision,' said Motormouth.

'We will sponsor you *just this once*.'

'But only for five p because of giving everything else to Oxfam.'

'For the starving children.'

Katy, in lordly fashion, thanked them for their generosity and said that every little helped.

'*However* pathetic.'

Caley tossed her head and said, 'So when are you doing this walk, anyway?'

'Tomorrow,' I said. 'In the lunch break.'

'How do we know it's genuine?'

When Caley said this, everybody groaned. We are

not the only people who think she and the Mouth are obnoxious. Someone said, 'Of course it's genuine! They're doing it for a sick horse.'

'I just wanted to make sure,' said Caley. 'That's all.'

'Yes, and who's going to check on them?' said Motormouth. 'There's got to be someone who checks on them!'

'We'll tell you,' I said. 'As soon as Rosie is safe! We'll let everyone know.'

'I didn't mean that, you idiot! I meant who's going to check the number of laps you do?'

Oh! We hadn't thought of that. But Mercy Humphries and Darren Bickerstaff said they would do it, so that was all right.

'I mean, I'd trust you, personally speaking,' said Darren. 'Some people just have suspicious minds.'

'No, but it ought to be official,' said Katy. 'That's why I'm keeping accounts.'

On the way home after school we had an idea and knocked on Mrs B's door.

'Excuse us for troubling you,' said Katy, 'but we wondered if you would feel like sponsoring us?'

'I daresay I could,' said Mrs B. 'So long as it's for a good cause.' She peered at the form I was holding out. 'What's it say? I can't read it... *Rescuing three-toed sloths from barbarian hordes?*'

I giggled at that but told her it was for a poor sick horse, so she wished us luck and put her name down for a pound, like Mr O'Sullivan. Katy and I really began to feel that our goal was in sight!

'I'm going to call my dad tonight,' said Katy, 'and see if he'll give us something.'

With great excitement she told me next morning that her dad had promised two pounds for every lap.

'We are definitely getting there!'

As soon as we could after we'd had our lunch we rushed to the playing field to begin the walk. Darren and Mercy sat solemnly side by side on a bench, with pen and paper, to record the number of laps.

I'd never realised quite how huge that playing field was until we started walking round it! The first lap took *eleven minutes.*

'We've got to go faster than this!' I said.

So then we speeded up and did the next lap in only nine.

'That's better!' I panted.

Round and round the playing field we pounded. Lots of people, by now, had come to watch and cheer us on. We didn't dare break into a run for fear some horrible person such as Motormouth would accuse us of cheating: 'It's meant to be a sponsored *walk!*'

'Bell's going in seven minutes,' warned Darren, as we completed our fifth lap.

'Think of Rosie, think of Rosie, think of Rosie!'

The words hammered through my brain as my feet hammered round the playing field. Left right, left right, think of Rosie, think of Rosie! Katy told me afterwards that she had been doing exactly the same thing.

'Bell!' shrieked Caley.

But we had made it! Six laps! Now all we had to do was collect the money…

Most people were really good; they came up to us at the end of the day and handed over what they had promised us. Just a few said they had forgotten and would bring it in next day, but we still staggered home with a huge pile of coins. We put it all in Katy's school bag. It weighed a ton!

After tea we counted it. It came to £54.14!

'And another £9.60 to come,' gloated Katy.

She snatched up the accounts and began busily writing.

Amount outstanding £127.00
Sponsered walk £74.14
Still to come £33.60*
Total £107.74
Amount still needed £19.26
* This includes £12 from Katy's dad

'Look!' She jabbed a triumphant finger. 'We're almost there!'

Almost, but not quite.

How were we going to get that last twenty pounds?

CHAPTER
7

Next day at school we collected the rest of the money that people owed us. Every single person paid up! Even Caley and the Mouth.

But the Mouth told us something that made us really angry. She told us that that hateful man at Farley Down hadn't had to pay a single penny for taking Rosie!

'He didn't pay *anything*. Mrs Foster let him take her for free, just to get rid of her. When I told her you were collecting money to buy her back she said you were being utterly stupid. He's conning you!'

Well! That was a bitter blow. That hideous man was just making money out of us.

Katy was so incensed she wanted to go racing out of

school right there and then to tell old Chislett what she thought of him.

'He's nothing but a rotten cheat!'

I said, 'He's worse than a cheat. He's a horse murderer.'

'So's Mrs Foster! She must have known what kind of person he was.'

'Course she did. They're all part of the horsey set. They all know each other.'

'He can't get away with this!' panted Katy.

She was striding up and down the field, practically frothing at the mouth.

'The awful thing is –' I said it glumly – 'he probably can.'

Rosie was his horse. He could ask whatever he liked for her.

'If we go and yell at him he might decide we can't have her at all. He might just send her to the knacker's. The *priority*,' I said, 'is to rescue Rosie.'

Once Katy had calmed down a bit, she could see that

I was right. We had to get that two hundred pounds before he changed his mind! I told Katy that as soon as Rosie was safe, she could go and yell at old Chislett as much as she wanted.

'I will!' said Katy. 'Don't you worry! I shall tell him I'm going to report him. I shall tell the newspapers. I shall tell everyone not to ride there. I shall—'

'Burst a blood vessel if you're not careful.'

That was the Mouth, strolling past with Caley.

'What does she think she knows about horses, anyway?' said Caley. 'Stupid townie!'

I tugged Katy away before she could get into a slanging match. We had more important things to think about! Such as where the last twenty pounds was going to come from.

'It's no use me asking Mum for more pocket money,' I said. 'I just know she won't give it to me.'

'Neither will mine,' said Katy. 'And she *won't* let me cash in my bonds. I've begged her and begged her, but she says it's for when I'm twenty-one. What good's that? I need it now!'

Rosie needed it now. Every minute she was in that horsey hell put her life in danger. *We had to get that money! But how?*

We racked our brains all the rest of the day. We racked them through French and history and double maths and even netball, and still nothing came.

'*Money!*' cried Katy, as we changed after netball. 'How do we get *money*?'

Someone said, 'Do a bank job!' and everyone giggled. Everyone except me and Katy.

'*Seriously*,' I said.

'You could always hold a raffle,' said Mercy Humphries.

'How?' I spun round eagerly. 'What do we have to do?'

'It's easy! You just get some prizes and write out some tickets and sell them at, say, fifty p each, and then pick the winning numbers out of a hat.'

'But how do you make *money*? If you have to buy prizes?'

'Well, mostly the prizes are given for free, which means you get to keep everything . . . You can make hundreds!'

Could it really be that simple?

No! Of course it couldn't. Nothing ever was, was it? Just as we were starting to grow enthusiastic a stupid know-it-all girl called Sheryl Stevens busybodily informed us that you couldn't hold raffles just like that.

'You have to have permission. Otherwise it's illegal.'

'Who says?' said Katy.

'It just is. It's against the law. As a matter of fact,' said the stupid busybody, 'what you did yesterday was probably against the law too.'

'What, walking round the playing field?'

'Getting people to give you money. My dad says it shouldn't have been allowed.'

We stared at her in dismay.

'We didn't *force* anyone,' said Katy.

'No, but you didn't have permission. It's all right *this* time, because I told him it was for a poor sick horse and that you're Animal Samaritans and it's your mission in life. But you'd better not try holding a raffle. Not unless you want to get done for it.'

It was horribly dispiriting. Katy and I discussed it as we made our way home.

'I thought it was supposed to be a free country,' I grumbled.

'That's what they *tell* you.'

'So why is it every time you just lift a finger to try and save a poor ill-treated animal they threaten to do you?'

'Obviously because it's *not* a free country,' fumed Katy. 'It's all full of stupid rules and regulations.'

'It's a pity the rules and regulations don't stop people torturing animals!'

As we turned into Honeypot Lane we saw old Mrs B and Sidney coming towards us. Sidney, as usual, waddled over for a cuddle.

'So how's it going?' said Mrs B. 'Have you managed to rescue that horse yet?'

Well! We didn't need a second invitation. We immediately skidded to a halt and poured out all our grievances, one after another. Mrs Foster, and Chislett, and Sheryl Stevens's dad, and how everything you tried to do turned out to be against the law unless it was torturing animals, which nobody except Katy and me seemed to care about.

'Not even our mums! They just groan and go, *oh, not again!*'

'Mine won't even let me have my own money that was given to me by my gran!'

'*Everybody* is against us,' I said.

'I know the feeling,' said Mrs B. 'It's a bit of a pig's ear, isn't it? How much have you managed to collect?'

'One hundred and eighty pounds and seventy-four p,' said Katy.

I don't know how she remembers these things! If it's not a round number it just goes right out of my mind.

Mrs B said that it sounded to her as if we had made a pretty good start.

'It's where to go next,' I said. 'If we can't hold a raffle…'

'I know one thing you could do,' said Mrs B. 'You

could help out an old lady with dodgy knees. How would you feel about walking Sidney for me every now and again? Say at the weekend? Just for a short while, give my aching bones a bit of a rest. What do you say? Fifteen pounds? Three weekends? Does that sound fair?'

Oh! It seemed more than fair. We would have walked Sidney without ever dreaming to ask for money! I even got as far as opening my mouth to say so, but fortunately Katy dug me in the ribs just in time.

'All right, then,' said Mrs B. 'We have a deal! I'll see you tomorrow. You can have the money up front, if you like. No point keeping you waiting.'

How I wish there were more people like Mrs B! Katy and I were positively jubilant!

'All we'll need now,' said Katy, 'is the odd twenty-six p.'

'Twenty-six p is *nothing*,' I said.

We could rescue Rosie this coming Saturday!

I told Benjy as soon as I got in.

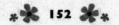

'We've got enough money to rescue the poor sick horse, and you were one of the people that helped! All those toys you gave us to sell… we couldn't have done it without you!'

Benjy was ever so pleased. He is quite a soft-hearted little boy. He wanted to know where we were going to keep the poor sick horse. He thought maybe in the back garden! I told him no, the garden wasn't big enough, she would need a proper stable – which reminded me we had never got around to ringing that horse sanctuary out at Spindle Down. We had been concentrating so hard on raising money that it had quite slipped our minds. The most important thing had been to get Rosie out of the hands of that hideous horrible man. We hadn't stopped to ask ourselves where she was going to go. We had to ring that sanctuary straight away!

'Mum,' I said, 'I'm just going round to Katy's.'

I thought that Katy might be better than me at ringing. Katy thought that I would be better than her.

'You're good at talking to people!'

'But you're better at arguing!'

'I don't see why we should have to argue,' said Katy. 'All you've got to do is just tell them we've rescued a horse.'

Well. That is what you would think. But things just never seem to work out the way you want them to.

First off, the sanctuary was FULL.

Second, all the people who took horses for them in emergencies were FULL.

Third, they seemed to think I was about six years old and didn't know what I was talking about.

Katy could see that I was getting more and more frustrated. She snatched the phone away from me.

'*Please!*' she begged. 'You've got to help us; this horse will die if you don't! She's got damaged lungs and they're riding her to death and we've raised all this money to rescue her and if you don't take her there's nowhere else she can go. WHAT ARE WE SUPPOSED TO DO?'

I stared at her, awestruck. I had never seen Katy like this! I had been trying so hard to be cool and calm and rational, and there was Katy practically having hysterics and it seemed they were listening to her because suddenly she cried, 'Oh, please! Please try!'

'What?' I said. 'What's happening?'

'They're going to ring round all the people they can think of and see if they can find someone who'll take her.'

'They're going to do it *now*?'

'Yes!'

'So when will they let us know?'

'Soon as they've found someone.'

Oh, please, I thought, *let it be soon!*

That was another night I didn't sleep. There are *lots* of sleepless nights when you're rescuing animals. There are just so many things to worry about. So many things to be upset about. Your head simply buzzes. I never tell Mum because I know if I did she'd only start on about school and about all this stress not being good for me.

'You won't be able to concentrate, Hannah, if you don't have your sleep.'

It was true that next day neither me nor Katy was in much of a concentrating mood but it wasn't because of not having enough sleep, it was because of thinking about Rosie and what would happen to her if the sanctuary couldn't find anyone to take her.

It wasn't till Friday that our minds were set at rest. By then I'd chewed my fingers practically to stumps and Katy had twisted her hair into so many knots she couldn't get a comb through it. Then on Friday afternoon when we got home Katy's mum said, 'Some horse person rang. A Mrs Broom. She wants you to call her.'

We rang immediately! Well, Katy did; I just listened. I didn't even have to strain my ears. Like lots of horsey people, Mrs Broom had a really LOUD sort of voice.

She said she lived in a place about three kilometres away called Church End.

'Don't really have room for another horse,' she barked. 'But needs must. Squeeze her in. Good-natured, is she?'

Katy said earnestly that Rosie was the sweetest, gentlest horse there ever was. Mrs Broom said, 'Great! That case, no problem. Call when you've got her. I'll drive over and pick her up.'

By then, Katy was almost sobbing with relief. She tried to say thank you, but Mrs Broom cut her short.

'No need for that. All in the same business. Love horses. Can't stand cruelty. Keep it up! Doing a grand job.'

It is *such* a comfort when you come across people that think the same way you do.

On Saturday morning I told Mum that Katy and I were going to walk Sidney to save Mrs B wearing her knees out.

'That's nice of you,' said Mum.

I didn't tell Mum that we were being paid for it. After all, we would quite happily have done it for free.

'Make sure you keep him on the lead,' warned Mum. 'You don't want him running off.'

'Mum, he's too old to go running off,' I said. 'He's nearly thirteen.' That is well into middle age in doggy years.

'Even an old dog can surprise you,' said Mum.

What did she know? She wasn't an animal person!

'Hannah, please, just don't take any chances,' said Mum. 'That dog is Mrs B's only companion. She'd be heartbroken if anything happened to him.'

'Nothing's going to happen to him,' I said. Honestly! Mums do fuss so.

Katy came whizzing out of her garden positively jubilant.

'Look, look!' She waved an envelope at me. 'Dad's money! He's sent it!'

She opened the envelope and showed me: two ten-pound notes, all crisp and clean and new.

'*Twenty pounds!*' I did a little jig of excitement. 'As soon as Mrs B pays us, we can go and rescue Rosie!'

I was a bit nervous about her carrying around so much money, but when I suggested that perhaps she ought to go back indoors and put it away with the rest she just gave a snorty sort of laugh, as if I was being ridiculous.

'It's perfectly *safe*. What d'you think? I'm going to lose it, or something?'

I didn't like to admit that the thought had crossed my mind.

'Don't worry.' She thrust it into one of the pockets of her jacket and pulled the zip. 'See? No one can get at it there. Let's work out a plan of campaign!'

We decided that what we would do, as soon as we had taken Sidney for his walk and got our fifteen pounds from Mrs B we would put all the money that we had collected into Katy's bumbag and go off to Farley Down to rescue Rosie! We would take her away from that horrible place and give her to lovely Mrs Broom.

It seemed like such a good idea. But oh, it all went disastrously wrong! It was partly my fault and partly

Katy's. But probably more my fault than hers. I should never have let Sidney off the lead! Mum had warned me, and I had taken no notice. I'd thought that being an Animal Samaritan I knew best. Only I didn't!

It was entirely my decision. Katy, very nobly, said afterwards that she should have stopped me but I expect I would only have argued. It seemed so safe! We were just pootling through the woods, with Sidney ambling along quite happily, stopping every now and then to investigate an interesting smell.

'I really don't see why he has to be kept on the lead,' I said. 'He's not going to go anywhere.'

Famous last words… We were just approaching the path leading out of the woods and I was about to put Sidney back on, because of a road coming up, when a big gingery cat suddenly leapt out of the bushes and went streaking off ahead of us – with Sidney streaking after him.

Mum was right! Even an old dog could take you by surprise.

I shrieked, '*SIDNEY!*' and went tearing after him. A car was parked at the kerb, with a woman pulling shopping bags out of the back. Just as she turned, her hands full of bags, the cat shot across her path and through a garden gate, Sidney panting wildly in pursuit. We watched in horror as he went walloping *crash bang* into the woman's legs. Next thing we knew, the woman was sprawled face down on the ground.

While I grabbed Sidney, Katy bravely tried to help the woman to her feet. Bravely, because that woman was really mad! I suppose anyone would have been. One of her hands was bleeding, and lots of shopping had tumbled out of her bags.

'I'm sorry! I'm so sorry!' panted Katy, as she snatched up tins and bottles and oh, God! A carton of eggs, all smashed and dripping.

'You ought to be sorry!' snapped the woman. 'Why was that dog not on a lead?'

Katy *could* have said it was because I had been stupid enough to let him off. Instead, she earnestly explained to the woman that we were walking Sidney for someone else and that we'd thought he was too old to go chasing after cats.

'Well, perhaps another time you'll know better!'

'I am so sorry, I am so sorry...' Katy was almost weeping. I just kept a tight hold on Sidney and tried to stop shaking. It was terrible, what had happened to the woman, but for a moment I'd been really scared that we'd have to go back and tell Mrs B we'd lost her beloved companion.

'You know, don't you,' said the woman, angrily snatching one of her shopping bags away from Katy, 'that it's against the law not to have a dangerous dog under control?'

'He's not dangerous!' sobbed Katy. 'He wouldn't hurt a fly!'

'I'm sure he'd have hurt my cat if he could have got hold of him. If I were to report this to the police—'

'Oh, please,' I begged, 'please don't! He belongs to an old lady and he's all she's got!'

'Well! Maybe I'll overlook it just this once,' said the woman. 'But on two conditions… one, you never *ever* take such a chance again. And two, you give me a contribution to my cat fund. It would seem the least you can do.'

I think we would have agreed to give her whatever she demanded. Anything to stop her going to the police!

'Very well,' said the woman. 'Just wait there.'

She went indoors and reappeared with a collecting tin that had the words **CRUMBLE DOWN CAT RESCUE** on it. She held it out.

Katy fumbled with the zip on her coat pocket. I saw her yank something out and stuff it into the tin. I was still too much in shock to say anything. I just wanted to turn and run!

'Thank you,' said the woman. She sounded a bit surprised. 'That's very generous of you!'

'What did you give her?' I hissed, as soon as we were safely out of reach.

'I don't know!' Katy looked at me, stricken.

'Count the money,' I said. 'Count the money!'

Katy had given the Crumble Down Cat Rescue the whole of the twenty pounds that her dad had sent for Rosie...

CHAPTER 8

It was our darkest hour. We had been so close! We could have rescued our darling Rosie from her hell hole that very afternoon. Poor Katy! She was so distressed. I kept telling her it wasn't her fault and that if I'd been the one holding the money I would probably have done the same. I didn't really, honestly think that I would, but it had after all been me who'd let Sidney off the lead so it wouldn't have been fair to lay all the blame at Katy's door. She was still riddled with guilt.

'I got in a panic,' she wept. 'All I could think of was having to tell Mrs B that the police had come and taken Sidney away! Or even worse, that he'd got run over!'

She scrubbed fiercely at her eyes. 'If Rosie dies it will be all because of me!'

'Well, it won't,' I said, 'because we're not going to let it happen! We're going to go and rescue her just like we said!'

'But how?' sobbed Katy. 'We're twenty pounds short! It'll take ages to make it up!'

'Wanna bet?' I said. 'We'll have it by this afternoon! And then we can ring Mrs Broom and tell her to come and get Rosie.'

Katy sniffed miserably. 'Where are we going to get it from?'

'I'll find a way!'

'But h—'

'Be quiet,' I said. 'I'm thinking!'

Ideas were fizzing through my head. I would take all my old clothes and all Benjy's old clothes and I would go back to the market and sell them, and never mind if Mum did find out and go raving mad. Rosie would be safe! That was all that mattered.

Except, unfortunately, our old clothes probably wouldn't fetch anywhere near twenty pounds. Not considering what they'd given us for my lovely china ornaments. We'd be lucky to get 20p.

Quick, quick, *think of something else!*

We could… go and sing in the shopping centre and have a cap for people to put money in!

We didn't have a cap. And we couldn't sing. They would most probably *stone* us.

Right! Well. We could…

'We could *collect* it!' I said.

'C-collect it? How?'

'Like the cat lady! She had a tin! That's what we'll do. We'll get a tin and we'll go into the shopping centre and we'll stand there and shake it and people will give us money. Quick!'

We raced home as fast as we could, which actually wasn't very fast at all. Sidney, safely back on the lead, simply dug in his heels and refused to be hurried. Without any cats to chase he just liked to amble and sniff and inspect every lamp post. We got there in the end and handed him over to Mrs B, who said that her knees were truly grateful for the rest.

'I can't tell you how lovely it is to have young people who are so reliable!'

We cringed a bit at that. We cringed even more when she beamingly pressed £15 into our hands.

'There! Now you can go and rescue your poor horse!'

'Do you think we should have told her?' said Katy, as we walked back up the lane. 'She might have given us some more money!' She clutched, suddenly, at my arm. 'We ought to go and tell her!'

'*No.*' I was horrified at the idea. Tell Mrs B that we had nearly lost her beloved dog? She would never trust us again! 'We've made a plan, let's just stick to it.'

I put my head round the back door and yelled at Mum that I was going round to Katy's. I didn't tell her that we were going into the shopping centre to ask people for money. I had a feeling it wasn't the sort of activity a mum would approve of. *You mind you don't get arrested! Just take care you don't get mugged!* et cetera and so forth.

Fortunately Katy's mum was out so we were able to ransack the cupboard for a suitable collecting pot without anyone asking awkward questions, such as, *What are you doing with that tin of peaches?*

'She's got loads of peaches,' said Katy 'She'll never miss just one.'

We took the top off with a special posh tin opener that Katy's mum has that doesn't leave jagged edges. Then we ate the peaches (it seemed silly to waste them) and washed the tin out. Then we found one of those plastic lids they sell for putting on tins that have been opened and cut a slit in it with a thing called a Stanley knife that Katy said her mum used for cutting carpet. Wow! Was it ever sharp. It sliced through the plastic like it was paper. A lethal weapon, if you ask me.

'Now we need some stickers,' I said. 'Two for us and one for the tin, so's people know what we're collecting for.'

This is the sticker we made for the tin:

HONEYPOT
HORSE RESCUE

Honeypot is the name of the lane where we live. It went really well with Horse Rescue!

For our own stickers Katy had a sudden burst of inspiration. On two large sheets of paper, in big, bold, felt-tip pen, she wrote:

PLEASE HELP US RESCUE ROSIE
A POOR SICK HORSE

Then she took two black bin liners, folded them in half, stuck the paper on them and fixed the bin liners to the front of our sweaters with safety pins. We were ready!

'I'm going to take *all* our money with us,' she said, 'so as soon as we've made up the twelve pounds we can go straight over to Farley Down and rescue Rosie!'

I was a bit nervous in case we might get mugged, but Katy said she would not only put the money in her bumbag but would hide the bumbag under a woolly sweater that her gran had made for her and that she'd never worn on account of it being about three sizes too big.

'See? Look! Nobody would ever know it was there.'

While we were waiting for the bus into town an elderly man came to join us. He was what Mum would call a whiskery colonel type. He peered at our tin and barked, 'So what's all this in aid of?' I shrank back, treading rather heavily on Katy's foot, and quavered that we were collecting money to save a sick horse.

'Are you, indeed?'

He glared at us from beneath huge bushy eyebrows. I honestly thought he was going to start telling us off. I don't know what I would have done if he'd barked at us again. I just suddenly felt like all the fight had gone out of me.

But then – oh, joy! He put a hand in his pocket,

produced a bunch of 10p pieces and gestured at me to hold out our tin. Gruffly he told us that we were 'Doing a good job! Hope this will help.'

'Oh, it will,' I said, 'it will! Thank you so much!'

We both felt incredibly encouraged by this. Even Katy began to cheer up and talk about being able to rescue Rosie that same afternoon. I thought that if everyone was like the whiskery colonel we would make up the money in no time!

But then we hit the shopping centre and our hearts quickly plummeted. First we stood in one place and then we stood in another, rattling our tin with its 10p pieces. *Nobody* put any money in it. Nobody even seemed to notice us.

'We should have brought two tins,' I said. 'Then we could have stood in different places.'

But Katy said she would be too scared to stand by herself and that it was more likely people would see us if we were together.

'I think this is the best spot,' she said. 'Near the fountain.'

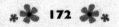

Well! If that was the best spot, I can't imagine what the worst would have been like. A whole hour went by and all we'd collected was about 50p! I started rattling the tin really hard and calling out to people as they passed.

'Help a sick horse! Please help a sick horse!'

A tiny child came wobbling over and made a simply huge display of giving us a 2p piece and then started whinging that we didn't have a 'sticky thing' for it to wear. The nerve of it!

'Honestly,' grumbled Katy, 'you'd think it had given us a fortune, the way it was carrying on.'

'Spoilt little brat,' I said.

Next thing we knew we had a rival. *Another* person with a tin came and stood right opposite us at the other side of the fountain.

'Cheek!' I said. 'We were here first! Go and see what they're collecting for.'

'You,' said Katy.

'I'm shaking the tin! Do you want to shake the tin?'

'No!' Katy backed away, horrified.

'So go and ask them what they're doing here. Tell them to move somewhere else. This is our spot!'

Very reluctantly, Katy set off. She reached the girl with the tin and I saw her saying something and then I saw the girl with the tin give me this cold, haughty stare as if I were a horrible icky fur ball sicked up by a cat. Katy turned, and started back. On the way, she suddenly stopped and peered at the fountain. I mean, really *peered*. It was like she'd never seen one before. I waved at her impatiently.

'Well! Did you tell her?' I said.

'Yes, but she said she was official and had every right to be there.'

'So have we! It's a free country, last I heard. What's she collecting for, anyway?'

'I don't know, I forgot to look. Something boring. People, or something. Listen, you know the fountain?' said Katy.

'What about it?'

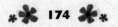

'It's got loads of money in it.'

'*Money?*'

'In the water. All coins. Just lying there.'

We exchanged glances. We didn't have to say anything. We both knew what the other was thinking: *it might SEEM like stealing, but if it was for Rosie…*

Slowly, we moved forward.

'Good,' I said. 'She seems to be going.'

'Quick, quick!' squeaked Katy. 'Before she turns round!'

It *wasn't* stealing. Whoever had put the coins in the water must have known they would be taken out again. They had probably meant for them to go to a good cause. And if rescuing a poor sick horse wasn't a good cause, I didn't know what was.

All the same, it seemed best not to take any chances. We'd already had one disaster. We didn't want another!

We kind of sauntered over to the fountain, trying to make like we just needed a bit of a rest. The fountain is in the shape of an enormous basin, with a rim that you can sit on. In the middle is a big stone fish, gushing water out of its mouth. And Katy was right: in the water, there was money! Lots of it. Coins of all kinds, just lying there.

'Try for the pounds and the fifties.' I said it out of the side of my mouth, just in case anyone was watching and could lip-read.

Katy nodded. All casual, she reached behind her with one hand and dipped it in the water. I did the same. My fingers had just closed on something that felt like a 50p when I saw our rival coming back. She was with a man. He was wearing a uniform...

My heart almost seized up. *Now* what?

'We're not stealing,' squeaked Katy. 'Hannah, tell them! We're not stealing!'

But the man didn't seem to have noticed that we were fishing for coins in the fountain. He seemed more interested in our collecting tin.

'You two,' he said. 'What do you think you're doing? This is private property! You have no right to collect money on these premises unless you have a permit. Which you do not.'

How did he know?

He knew because he was a security guard. I'd heard about the security guards. Darren Bickerstaff, who is a boy in our class, had told me. He'd said they could arrest you on the spot! You didn't even have to be *doing* anything. Just walking round minding your own business.

'We were just trying to get some money to help a poor sick horse,' I stammered.

'Well, you go somewhere else and do it. Not in here.'

'They're not allowed, anyway!' shrieked the girl with the tin. 'They're underage! It's illegal!'

That was when we really drooped. It was like all the stuffing had been knocked out of us. It didn't matter what we tried to do, it seemed there was always some law against it. We couldn't hold a raffle, we couldn't collect, we weren't even supposed to have gone on our sponsored walk. We both felt utterly dejected.

And then something happened that I can only describe as a miracle. This lady was walking past. We didn't recognise her at first – but she recognised us! She stopped and said, 'Oh dear! In trouble *again*?'

It was the cat lady! The one Katy had given all her dad's money to!

'What's the problem this time?' she said.

She didn't sound angry; more like sorry for us. Glumly I explained how we were trying to collect money to rescue Rosie.

'We thought we'd make a tin like your cat one, but they won't let us.'

'They won't let us do *anything*,' said Katy.

'Whatever we try, they say it's illegal!'

'Alas,' said the cat lady, 'that is bewrockrissy for you.'

Well, that is what I *thought* she said. It was what it sounded like. I have since discovered that it is spelt b.u.r.e.a.u.c.r.a.c.y., and that what it means is rules and regulations and bunches of people telling you that you're not allowed to do things.

'I fear,' said the cat lady, 'that making money is never easy.'

'We had enough before Sidney went and chased your cat!' It came bursting out of me before I could stop it.

I didn't mean to sound accusing, but Katy immediately burst into tears and cried, 'Oh, please! Please don't! Rosie's going to die and it's all my fault!'

The cat lady said, 'Why is it all your fault?'

'It's not,' I said. 'It's both our faults.'

Before I knew it, I was telling her the whole sad story.

'I thought he'd be all right, I thought he was too old to do anything silly, so I took him off the lead—'

'And I gave you the twenty pounds that my dad had given us because I was in a panic and now we don't have enough left!' The tears came welling up in Katy's eyes all over again. They were already pink from the crying she'd done earlier.

'Ah.' The cat lady nodded. 'That begins to make sense! I did wonder why you were so generous. I only meant you to put fifty p in the pot. I just wanted to teach you a lesson, not rob you!'

'We robbed Rosie,' sobbed Katy. 'We've robbed her of her life!'

'Now, now, don't be overdramatic.' The cat lady said it briskly. She was quite a brisk sort of person. 'All is not yet lost! Where exactly is she, this horse of yours?'

I told her that she was at Farley Down, and the cat lady raised her eyebrows.

'That place! It should have been shut down years ago. So, they're flogging this poor animal to death but if you can manage to raise enough money you can rescue her. Only now you're twenty pounds short. Well! Let's see if we can't think of a solution... suppose you give me what you've got in that tin, and in return I'll give you your twenty pounds back. How does that strike you?'

Katy said 'Oh!' and clapped both hands to her mouth. I think she just couldn't believe it. Someone was actually being *nice* to us!

I said 'Oh!' as well. But instead of clapping my hands

to my mouth, I thrust our tin at the cat lady. 'That means we could go and rescue her straight away!'

'How do you propose to get there?' said the cat lady. 'It's a fair old distance. Would you like me to drive you?'

Better and better! Sometimes you feel that there *is* some justice in the world.

But Katy was plucking at me. 'Hannah... you don't think—'

'What?'

'We ought to ring home?'

I was about to say *no* – I just wanted to go and get Rosie – when the cat lady stepped in.

'Certainly you ought! You should always ring home. Do it straight away.'

I pulled a face at Katy. Her and her stupid ideas! It was all wasting valuable time. As it happened, neither of our mums was in, so we simply left messages. Katy said that at least it would stop them worrying. I thought yes, and it could mean we arrived too late. I didn't say so, however. Katy was already feeling quite guilty enough.

'Come on, then!' said the cat lady. 'Get rid of your bin liners and we'll go and rescue a horse!'

The cat lady's car had stickers all over it – **CATS PROTECTION**, and **CRUMBLE DOWN CAT RESCUE** – and smelt a bit catty in a warm, cosy sort of way.

The cat lady's name was Miss Hatterman and as it turned out it was just as well she was with us. I don't know what we would have done if she hadn't been. We might even have simply given up and crept away, defeated. I certainly *hope* we wouldn't, but we were just feeling so bruised and battered.

When we got to the stables Miss Hatterman said she had better come in with us, 'Just in case.' I think she meant just in case old Chislett tried to cheat us – which is exactly what he did.

For a start, Rosie wasn't there. She'd been sent on another hack…

Katy clutched at my arm. I could feel her fingers digging into me.

'I thought, according to these young girls,' said Miss Hatterman, 'this particular horse was not fit to be taken on hacks?'

'These two young girls ought to mind their own poxy business!' snarled old Chislett. 'Apart from anything else, they haven't the faintest idea what they're talking about!'

'Well, there's a perfectly easy way to find out,' said Miss Hatterman. 'We can always call a vet to come and examine the horse. See what he says.'

'You do that,' agreed the horrible man. 'He'll tell you what I'm telling you... that horse is as fit as any other so long as it's ridden quietly.'

'She wasn't ridden quietly last time!' I cried. 'She came back all in a lather!'

'Yes, and she was being *cantered*,' said Katy. 'We saw her!'

'Did you, now?'

'Yes, we did! And she shouldn't be, she's got damaged lungs!'

Katy turned desperately to Miss Hatterman. We

were terrified she would choose to believe old Chislett rather than us. Grown-ups almost always side with each other against young people. But Miss Hatterman obviously didn't like old Chislett – well, I don't really see how anyone could, the way he kept shouting swear words all over the place.

'I believe you agreed that if these girls could raise sufficient money, you would let them take the horse away.'

A look of extreme cunning came over the Chislett's face. 'I might have done. Might not have done.'

'Did you, or didn't you?' said Miss Hatterman.

'What if I did?'

'We've got the money!' Katy pulled up her sweater to show him her bumbag, but Miss Hatterman put out a hand to stop her.

'Not until we see the horse.'

'Well, you can't see the horse because it's not poxy well here! What do you think I am? A poxy magician? In any case, I've changed my mind. You can keep your money. I'll keep the horse.'

The Chislett went striding off, all bow-legged and belligerent, across the yard.

'You can't do this!' I shouted. 'We had an agreement!'

'You think I give a toss?' The Chislett turned and made a rude sign. A *really* rude sign. 'Get out of my yard or I'll have you up for trespassing!'

'Charming,' murmured Miss Hatterman.

'We *did* have an agreement,' I said.

'Oh, I believe you! Don't worry, we're not letting this go. Let us see –' Miss Hatterman beckoned imperiously to a girl who had just emerged from one of the boxes – 'if we can prise out a bit more information.'

The girl came up. She wasn't much older than us and she was looking really scared.

'It's all right, I'm not going to eat you,' said Miss Hatterman. But I don't think it was Miss Hatterman she was scared of; I think it was old Chislett. 'We'd just like to know where the ride has gone.'

The girl gave a fearful glance back over her shoulder.

'To the Gallops,' she muttered.

The Gallops! My heart sank like a block of cement. Everyone – unless they were complete beginners – took the Gallops at full tilt.

'Oh no,' whispered Katy. She had turned sheet-white. For just a moment I really thought she was going to faint.

'Come!' Miss Hatterman led the way back to her car. 'Let us go and intercept them!'

Miss Hatterman was quite old – at least seventy, I should think – but she drove that car like she was some kind of racing driver. As we reached the Gallops we could see the ride strung out along its length. Even those poor knackered horses from Farley Down were flogged at full stretch along the Gallops.

'Where's your one?' said Miss Hatterman. 'Can you see her?'

'N-no,' quavered Katy. And then, '*Yes!* She's right up at the front!'

The big red-faced man was riding her. He had a crop, and he was thrashing Rosie with it, to make her go.

Katy screamed. I stuffed my fist in my mouth.

Miss Hatterman, grim-faced, said, 'We'll put a stop to this!'

She stepped on the gas and the car shot down the road that ran alongside. We soon overtook the horses. But even as we drew to a halt, Rosie stumbled and fell.

She did not get up again.

We were too late!

CHAPTER 9

Miss Hatterman brought the car to a stop. Katy and I went stumbling out.

'Rosie!' I cried. 'Oh, Rosie!'

I fell to my knees beside her. That poor, gentle, trusting horse, killed by the greed and cruelty of human beings!

Katy knelt down next to me. Tears were streaming from her eyes.

The red-faced man had come off when Rosie fell. He had gone sprawling. Served him right! Maybe he had broken his neck. Who cared?

Rosie was all we cared about! Our dear, sweet, darling Rosie. She had been through so much in her life! Caught in a fire, terrified and unable to escape. She should have been allowed to live out her remaining years in a lush green meadow, with some horsey friends. Not be ridden to death by some horrible brute of a man, thrashing at her, terrifying her, digging his heels into her poor suffering body.

All the other riders had pulled up. They sat there, white-faced, staring at that big, brave, beautiful horse lying so still on the ground. Natalie was the only one who dismounted. She handed the reins to someone and came over.

'We told you!' sobbed Katy. 'We told you!'

The red-faced man had picked himself up.

'I wasn't to know! How was I to know? Jeff said she was okay! He said she was just lazy. How was I to know?'

I opened my mouth to yell something but became suddenly aware that Katy was tugging at my sleeve. 'Hannah!' she gasped. 'Look!'

I didn't want to look. I simply couldn't bear it.

'Look!' shrieked Hannah.

I forced myself to do so. 'Oh!'

Rosie was still with us! Her eyes had opened and her flanks had started to heave as she struggled for breath. But her eyes were rolling, and her breath came in long, rattling gasps.

Katy and I crouched there, murmuring to her, urgently but softly, so that only she could hear.

'Darling Rosie! Please don't die! We love you so much! We've fought so hard! Please, Rosie! Stay with us!'

Of course we knew she couldn't understand what we were saying. But she was a poor sick animal in distress and all we could hope was that the sound of our voices, whispering in her ear, and the feel of our hands, gently stroking and soothing, would bring her some comfort and give her the will to keep fighting.

I have no idea what Natalie was doing all this time. Just standing there, I guess; I didn't bother to look. I was too concerned with our poor Rosie, trying to ease her suffering.

After what seemed like ages, though it was probably

only a few minutes, Rosie started to make feeble attempts to get back on her feet. We didn't know whether to help her or try to keep her still. If she wanted to get up, then surely that must be a good sign?

But suppose the strain proved too much?

We didn't know what to do!

It was Miss Hatterman who came to our aid. Not Natalie, who should have been the one. After all, she was in charge of the ride. She was supposed to know about horses. But she was just standing there, looking dazed. As if for the first time she was accepting that everything we'd told her had been true. Rosie *did* have damaged lungs and she *shouldn't* have been ridden.

Miss Hatterman said, 'Easy, now! Take it easy, sweetheart!' And then she helped us – ever so gently – get Rosie back up. It seemed to be what she wanted to do. They always say that animals know what is best for themselves, the way that dogs, for instance, will eat grass if they are feeling sick, so maybe you have to let them choose.

'Where was it you were planning to take her?' said Miss Hatterman.

We explained that we had to telephone Mrs Broom so that she could come with her horsebox.

Miss Hatterman said, 'Right. Give me her number! I'll call her straight away.'

Natalie suddenly sprang back into life. 'Excuse me,' she said. 'This horse belongs to my father.'

Miss Hatterman regarded her coldly. 'In that case, young woman, your father should be ashamed of himself. He'll be lucky if he doesn't face a prosecution.'

That shut her up!

By now, all the other riders had dismounted and were standing around in a huddle. Red Face was still insisting, to anyone who would listen, that it wasn't his fault: 'Jeff said she was okay!'

It was true that old Chislett *had* tried making out that Rosie was fit enough to be ridden, so maybe I should have felt at least a little bit sorry for poor old Red Face. I should think it would haunt you all your life long, knowing that you have flogged and whipped and beaten a noble animal almost to death. But all my sympathies were with Rosie; I didn't have any to spare for the person who had caused her such agony.

Katy and I crouched by her side as she struggled for breath. Her ears were pulled back, her lips stretched over her teeth and her poor eyes were still rolling in their sockets. Horrid foamy stuff was coming out of her nostrils, and her flanks heaved painfully with the effort of trying to get enough air into her lungs. She was trembling all over, and the sweat was pouring off her.

I said to Natalie, 'She'll get cold! We should wipe her!'

Natalie just shook her head, helplessly, as if to say, 'What with?' I think she cared; sort of. She wasn't totally heartless. But she was just so shocked by what had happened. She had this glazed expression in her eyes. Perhaps she hadn't realised until now how cruel and grasping her dad really was.

Rosie suddenly threw her head into the air then let it sink back down again between her shoulders.

'Let's take her saddle off,' said Katy.

That was a good idea, and one that I should have thought of. Gently we removed the saddle, and the saddle blanket as well, because it was drenched in sweat. We had to find something to wipe her with!

'Here,' said Miss Hatterman. 'Put this over her.' She had brought a rug from the car, a lovely warm tartan rug! 'How is she doing?' She took hold of Rosie's bridle and gently stroked her neck. 'Poor girl! You're very distressed, aren't you? Don't worry! We'll soon have you tucked into a nice cosy stall and the vet will come and see you.'

It is so lovely when a grown-up person talks to animals the way that me and Katy do! Most grown-ups are too embarrassed; they think it makes them look silly. It didn't bother Miss Hatterman one little bit! She probably talked to her cats like that.

'Your Mrs Broom is on her way,' she said. 'She'll be here in a few minutes.'

You will simply never guess what happened next. There was a loud screech of brakes and a car pulled up. It was old Chislett! He came roaring over, waving his arms like a windmill and screaming four-letter words, a great long spew of them.

'What the devil is going on here? What have you done to that poxy horse? And what are you poxy kids doing?'

'They're taking her to a sanctuary.' That was Natalie. She sounded quite defiant. I couldn't believe it! Suddenly she was on our side. 'They've got someone coming to take her away.'

'My ****** horse!' screamed Chislett. 'That's my ****** horse!'

Miss Hatterman stepped forward, placing herself protectively in front of us.

'It is no longer your horse,' she said. 'It is our horse. And if you give us any trouble, we shall bring a prosecution.'

Old Chislett had gone so purple in the face I thought he was going to explode. Either that, or give Miss

Hatterman a black eye. And then a truly surprising thing happened. The red-faced man came barrelling over. He grabbed hold of the Chislett's collar and began shaking him to and fro.

'You told me that horse was fit to be ridden! You gave me your word! You said if it didn't go, then to give it some stick. You said it was just lazy. Now look at it! Look at the state of it!'

He lifted old Chislett off the ground and swung him round, like a puppet, so that he was forced to look at Rosie.

'Collapsed, didn't it? With me on top of it! I could have broken my neck!'

'Yes, and the horse could have died!' That was another of the riders, a woman, deciding to join in. 'You must have known it wasn't fit!'

'He had no right sending it out like that!'

'Shouldn't be allowed to keep horses if that's the way he treats them!'

They were all at it now, all ganging up on old Chislett.

It was about time! He didn't run a stables, he ran a prison. All his horses were knackered. They weren't fed properly, they weren't looked after properly, and now he'd almost managed to kill our poor Rosie.

A horsebox had drawn up behind Miss Hatterman's car. A big woman wearing stretchy riding breeches and a rollneck sweater under a bright yellow fleece got out of it and came running over.

'This the horse? Let me have a look at her!' She crouched down beside Rosie. 'Oh, my poor baby! You poor, poor baby! What have they been doing to you?'

'Riding her to death!' I said.

'Yes! It looks like it.'

She ran her hands over Rosie's trembling flanks. You could just tell from the way she did it that she knew about horses. For the first time I felt a faint glimmer of hope.

'Is she going to be all right?' whispered Katy.

'Get her back to my place. Already rung the vet. Should be there to meet us.'

With such tenderness, step by faltering step, she coaxed Rosie towards the horsebox. Old Chislett didn't say a word, not even a four-letter one. Some of the riders were muttering about reporting him to the RSPCA. Even his own daughter wouldn't speak up for him. That mean, miserable man had had his day!

We helped lead Rosie up the ramp. She was still very wobbly, but she was so brave! Mrs Broom said that if we liked we could stay with her. She said it would help keep her calm if we were there.

We remembered, just in time, to call our thanks to Mrs Hatterman for all that she'd done.

'Ring me,' she said. 'Let me know what happens.'

We promised that we would.

All the way to Mrs Broom's place we whispered words of encouragement to Rosie, telling her what a brave girl she was, and how she was going to be looked after. Katy remembered what Bethany had once told us, about how you could communicate with horses by gently blowing up their nostrils. She tried it with Rosie and

Rosie twitched an ear to show us that she knew we were there. I kept stroking her, trying to stop her trembling, trying to reassure her that nothing else bad was going to happen to her. I was terrified she might think she was going to the knacker's yard. It made me go cold all over to reflect that this was almost certainly what would have happened if Katy and I – and Miss Hatterman – hadn't turned up when we did.

The vet was there waiting for us as we drove into Mrs Broom's yard. Mrs Broom said that as Rosie knew us we should be the ones to introduce her to her new home. We made it as easy for her as we possibly could, murmuring softly to her as we led her across the yard and into the sweet-smelling box, big and airy, with a bed of fresh straw that had been prepared for her. She was so good, and so docile! All she wanted to do – all she'd ever wanted to do – was just to please people.

We would have given anything to be able to stay until the vet had finished, but Mrs Broom warned us that he might be there some time. She told us that Rosie was a very sick horse.

'It won't be quick or easy. But, rest assured, I'll call you the minute there's any news.'

With that, sadly, we had to be content. We kissed Rosie goodbye and set off on the long journey home. We had to take a bus as far as Crumble Down, and then walk back across the fields.

Needless to say, Mum was in a state, wondering what had happened.

'I got your message,' she said. 'Where on earth have you been?'

'We went to rescue Rosie,' I said. 'Mum, she's safe! A lovely lady has taken her! She's got this sanctuary out at Church End, and she's promised to do everything she can!'

'Well, that is excellent news,' said Mum. 'Well done, the pair of you! You've worked really hard. I'm so pleased!'

I basked happily in Mum's approval – which lasted about two seconds! And then she said, 'It would be nice to think that now, maybe, life could return to normal? Whatever passes for normal, with you two. This week a horse, next week, a hippopotamus… who knows?'

We *would* rescue a hippopotamus. Of course we would! If we ever came across one that was in trouble.

We were just finishing tea when my phone rang. Mum doesn't like me answering the phone when we're eating, but she didn't say anything when I snatched it up. She knew I was desperately waiting to hear about Rosie.

'Katy?' I suddenly found that I had gone all weak and trembly. 'Did she ring?'

Katy said, 'Yes! She just called. Rosie's going to be all right!'

I gave a short scream and jubilantly punched the air.

'She said we can go and see her whenever we want, maybe next Saturday, and do you want to ring Miss Hatterman or shall I do it?'

I said that I would do it as I really like giving good news to people. I asked Mum if I could do it immediately, and Mum said, 'Yes, go on, you've deserved it.'

Miss Hatterman seemed almost as pleased as me and Katy.

'Wonderful!' she said. 'Absolutely wonderful! And by the way,' she added, 'you'll be relieved to hear I have taken steps to have that dreadful place shut down and that one of the big sanctuaries has agreed to take the horses. So whatever you do, don't give a penny piece to that man. *Not one penny.* Do you hear?'

It was only then that I remembered… we had more than two hundred pounds that we didn't need any more! I rang Katy back as soon as we'd finished tea and we discussed what to do with it. We decided it was only right it should go to Mrs Broom for looking after Rosie.

We agreed that we would hand it over the following Sunday, before we went for our ride. What we would do, we decided, was take Benjy with us, then we could drop him off at home, collect our bikes and whizz up to the stables. Katy agreed that Benjy deserved the chance to say hello to Rosie, since he had, after all, done his best to help when we were trying to raise money. I'd told her how he'd staggered into my room with his arms full of clothes that he thought we could sell. And then, when I'd said that Mum wouldn't approve, he'd gone and got some of his toys. It wasn't every little boy that would do that!

I asked him if he would like to come with us. 'We're going to visit the poor sick horse that you helped us rescue.'

He was so proud when I said that. He importantly told Mum: 'Going to vithit the poor thick horth that I helped rethcue!'

We should have been happy, that Sunday. We *were* happy, to begin with. Just sitting there on the bus, the three of us, on our way to see Rosie. I don't know *how* Katy and I managed to fall out with each other. We never fall out! We're above that sort of thing. We're Animal Samaritans, and animals come first. We don't have time for quarrelling.

I can't remember which of us started it. It may have been Katy; it may have been me. I think I said something about making sure we didn't turn up late for our ride, and Katy then pointed out that we hadn't actually booked for a ride.

I said, 'No, but they'll be expecting us. We always go on a Sunday.'

Katy reminded me that we hadn't gone last Sunday. '*Or* the Sunday before. That was when you made us go to Farley Down.'

'Oh.' I'd forgotten that. And it had been my idea! 'In that case,' I said, 'I'd better call them right now.' I pulled out my phone. 'What's the number? Can you remember?'

Katy *always* remembers numbers. I waited impatiently, but quite suddenly she burst out, 'I'm not sure we ought to be doing it!'

'Doing what?' I said.

'*Riding*,' said Katy.

Well, so that was how it started. But whether it was my fault or Katy's that we ended up being so horrid to each other, I am not absolutely certain.

I remember Katy saying that riding was okay if you

owned your own horse, because then you could be sure it was being properly looked after and not ridden into the ground or kept in a horrible dark prison cell. Also, she said, it wouldn't be sent for horsemeat if it got sick, or sold to someone else if you got too big for it.

I remember saying that I agreed with her, but that if people like us didn't go to riding schools there wouldn't *be* any riding schools, and what did she think would happen to all the poor horses?

Katy then said something about too many horses being bred anyway – 'Half of them end up as horsemeat' – and I said, 'Well, *all* of them would end up as horsemeat if you had your way!'

So then Katy accused me of not caring about the welfare of horses but only about my own selfish pleasure.

'Just because you like riding, you try to pretend it's all right!'

Well! That made me really cross. So in return I told

her that she only wanted to stop because she didn't enjoy it.

'Because basically you're scared!'

I suppose it was rather nasty of me. But *she* had accused me of being selfish!

After that, it all went to pieces. Poor Benjy kept looking from one of us to the other, obviously trying to work out what was making us so cross. We'd started out so happily! By the time we reached Mrs Broom's we were hardly on speaking terms. And then we saw Rosie, our big, brave, beautiful horse! And all of a sudden our anger just melted away.

You can't be mad at each other when you both love animals. It is just such a waste of energy.

Rosie was in her box, standing there with her big horsey head hanging over the top of the door. When she saw us her ears pricked up and she made a little excited whinnying sound.

'She recognises us!' cried Katy.

'Well, of course she does,' said Mrs Broom. 'Horses

aren't stupid! They always remember the people who love them.'

I asked whether we could give her an apple, and Mrs Broom said that we could, so we went into her box and held out two big juicy apples that we had brought with us and while she was eating them we cuddled and crooned, and Rosie rubbed her head against us and then did her old trick of nuzzling our pockets in case we had more titbits. And of course we'd put some in there, just in case. I had a carrot, and Katy had a biscuit. Benjy was upset because he didn't have anything, so I broke my carrot in half for him and he giggled delightedly as Rosie very gently closed her lips over it.

It was so heart-warming! She was looking like her old self again. Her head was up, her coat was shiny, she was interested in all that was going on around her. She still trusted human beings in spite of all that she had suffered.

'But you won't ever suffer again,' I whispered.

Mrs Broom said that next week she would turn her out into the paddock with her other rescues.

'She'll lead the good life from now on.'

We gave Mrs Broom the money we had collected and she was really grateful. It made it seem all worthwhile! We forgot the horrid things that had happened: old Chislett swearing at us, and the security guard threatening us, and the Mouth sneering at us, calling us stupid townies. Our darling Rosie was safe, and that was all that mattered.

It's moments like that when you know you'll always fight for animals. You'll go on rescuing them, no matter what. Once you've started, it's impossible to stop.

We finally, reluctantly, had to tear ourselves away. We both said our goodbyes to Rosie. Katy blew up her nose and kissed her: I wobbled her big rubbery lip with my finger. Benjy, not being able to reach that far, wrapped his arms round one of her legs! It wasn't something you could safely do with many horses, but with Rosie we didn't even hold our breath. She was the gentlest horse ever! We promised that we would come back very soon and visit her.

'Though I expect,' said Katy, 'once she's out in the paddock she'll find herself a handsome horsey boyfriend and forget all about us.'

'She may well find a boyfriend,' agreed Mrs Broom, 'but she'll never forget you.'

The three of us set off back down the track, towards the main road and the bus stop. Katy and I were silent for a while, then suddenly we both spoke together.

'I'm really sorry I—'

We stopped.

'After you.'

We said that together too!

'I'm really sorry I said you were scared,' I said.

'I'm sorry I said you were selfish,' said Katy.

'Well, but I probably am.' I sighed. This was a BIG DECISION I was about to take. 'You're right, I'm just thinking about me. Not the horses. Maybe I ought to stop doing it.'

'Hannah, no!' cried Katy. 'It's important you *don't* stop. Because if you stop you won't know what's going on, and if you don't know what's going on then it's like closing your eyes to the truth. It means you don't have to do anything about it, which is a whole lot easier than having to fight, and stand up to people like old Chislett and get shouted at and sworn at. When I actually stop to think about it,' she said, 'it's your duty *not* to stop.'

I looked at her uncertainly. 'You really mean it?'

'I do,' said Katy.

I struggled for a moment with my conscience, before deciding – much to my relief! – that she was probably right.

'Except that if it's *my* duty,' I said, 'it has to be yours as well. After all, we've both sworn to help animals! I can't do it all by myself.'

It was Katy's turn to struggle.

'Okay,' she said. 'We'll both carry on. Though I'm sure,' she added, 'it won't just be horses we have to help. It'll be dogs and cats and – and donkeys and—'

'Hippopotamutheth!' cried Benjy.

I said, 'Yeah, right… hippopotamuses. We're just

as likely to bump into a hippopotamus in the middle of the road!'

Katy giggled. 'What would you do if we did? If we just happened to be walking along, minding our own business, and suddenly found one standing there?'

Promptly I said, 'Check to see if it had a collar!'

'And what if it didn't?'

'Then I'd... I'd look on the computer and see if I could find a hippotamus sanctuary!'

'Or maybe just ring a zoo?' said Katy.

'Well... yes.' I said it rather reluctantly. It didn't seem very imaginative. 'I suppose we could just ring a zoo.'

'So long as we did *something*.'

'We'd always do *something*.'

'I mean, you couldn't just leave it in the middle of the road.'

I looked at her witheringly. 'Animal Samaritans,' I said, 'do not leave hippopotamuses in the middle of roads.'

In the meantime we both agreed that it would be a relief, after all the hard work we'd put in, to have a bit of a break from constantly racking our brains how to rescue some poor ill-used animal that needed our help.

'Let's just hope,' said Katy, 'that we don't find anything today.'

Especially not a hippopotamus.

The first in a brand-new series about dancing, friendship and following your dreams from best-loved author Jean Ure, whose books are described by Jacqueline Wilson as 'funny, funky, feisty – and fantastic reads!'

When new girl Caitlyn arrives at Coombe House School Maddy is sure she must be a fellow ballet dancer; she certainly has all the grace and poise of a ballerina. So when Caitlyn denies it, Maddy isn't convinced. But it isn't until she comes across Caitlyn practising ballet in the gym that she realises there must be more to her story… Just what can it be? Maddy is determined to find out!

The second story in a new series about dancing, friendship and following your dreams from best-loved author Jean Ure, whose books are described by Jacqueline Wilson as 'funny, funky, feisty – and fantastic reads!'

Maddy is delighted when she and her friends are accepted to the prestigious City Ballet School – it feels like one step closer to their dream of becoming professional dancers. But the school brings a whole new set of challenges – and soon Maddy finds herself tested like never before.

The final instalment in this inspiring series about dancing, friendship and following your dreams!

A big performance looms and Maddy knows that the school has a way of weeding out the weakest dancers. Now is her time to shine. But will Maddy and her friends be celebrating at the end of the year?